# Pilgrims of Death

Elkin Echeverri

Half Moon Press

Copyright © 2008 Elkin Echeverri
All rights reserved.
www.elkinecheverri.com

Translation from Spanish to English: Maria Florez
Cover Art: Arturo Velasquez
Photography: Arturo Velasquez
Photomar Studio / www.photomar.com
Cover Art Models: Gloria Porras & Elkin Echeverri

Published in the United States by Half Moon Press.

No part of this book may be reproduced or utilized in any form or by any means, electronic or mechanical, including photocopying, recording, or by any information storage and retrieval system without permission in writing from the publisher.

*To Camila*
*The Light of my Soul*

# Index

| | |
|---|---|
| ONE | 11 |
| TWO | 17 |
| THREE | 26 |
| FOUR | 32 |
| FIVE | 36 |
| SIX | 39 |
| SEVEN | 46 |
| EIGHT | 54 |
| NINE | 60 |
| TEN | 64 |
| ELEVEN | 73 |
| TWELVE | 76 |

| | |
|---|---|
| THIRTEEN | 83 |
| FOURTEEN | 91 |
| FIFTEEN | 96 |
| SIXTEEN | 101 |
| SEVENTEEN | 105 |
| EIGHTEEN | 115 |
| NINETEEN | 122 |
| TWENTY | 130 |
| TWENTY ONE | 136 |
| TWENTY TWO | 140 |
| TWENTY THREE | 144 |

# PILGRIMS OF DEATH

## ONE

When the Boss called Mauro to tell him that he needed 'a small job' done, of those he already knew, he wasn't surprised at all. But if he had known what it was about, he would have probably wished not to have accepted the offer made to him.

Mauro was a guy who did not believe in omens; he was one of those men who never lacked a drink or a motive to get rid of any mortal. He had earned the reputation of fearless and tough, thanks to the many shootings of which he had come out untouched.

"I am protected by the devil himself," he used to say, with a worry-less gesture.

Mauro; with no last names, no address, no past, and sometimes, depending on his state of mind, with no future. This was the same he would want anybody to say about him. A Holy Friday, he said, pointing with a large 38 at his face that he already smelled like the deccased before being born

Mauro was twenty two years old and was some kind of lucky charm for the neighborhood, since only a few men

# ✠ Pilgrims of Death

like him had been able to get to his age alive. There were those who lived beyond the barrier of twenty two, like *Gárgaras* or *Pierna loca*, who were twenty five and thirty respectively, but from a few years back were getting around in wheel chairs. Living to kill others was a very tough business, and when a young man got himself in that labyrinth of fear and misery, he would hardly come out of it unharmed at the other end of the tunnel.

Mauro: a lucky charm, a relic, clownish or womanizer; a murderer or altar boy. It did not matter how he was recognized; what he cared about was that he had been able to maintain himself available in the list of favorites of organized crime and even in that of the non-organized. Tall and strong, due to so many beatings and sorrows, beautiful, flirtatious and kind; that is how he was. Feared or admired; all depended on what side of arms he was. That's how he was; with a heart so big that it didn't fit in his chest.

He liked to read the comics, watch rock concerts; he used to love to enjoy percussion and the base drilling a hole in his soul, grinding his sorrows. It was his way to let off steam; music was his clandestine lover, his favorite

# PILGRIMS OF DEATH

woman. He felt able to stand up any girlfriend, in order to feel in his veins the constant pumping of the music. Because as a boyfriend, Mauro was so cynic that he used to succeed in having three and even four girlfriends in the same block! "Just friends," he used to say, when the environment would become heavy with other girls in the same sector.

Mauro, 'the man with seven lives', was not happy with one woman at a time. He spent his time presuming of his manhood, but he never let any of his lovers' names escape, not even if he were drunk. He was a gentleman until the definition of the word would allow him. Even at the time of executing someone, he would respect him without consideration. He did not hesitate in prolonging a 'business deal', but the client – the one who paid – as well as the future deceased – the one who received – ought to remain satisfied with his job.

And it was this reckless way of seeing life which saved his life in more than one occasion, and it was because of this that the 'tough ones' would entrust him with the hardest jobs. There was no 'twisted man' too complicated to throw on the ground, nor was there a mess he didn't feel

# Pilgrims of Death

capable of straightening out because he would confront anything, and he would knock down anything that would come in front of him.

The afternoon his boss called him to propose 'a deal', he took his sweet little time to show up to the appointment. He went to the store of la señora Adela, bought a new shirt for him, and even a new lotion, "because one could not appear in front of the boss wearing rags."

He took his DT, the motorcycle someone had given him for having sent *Tato* to the 'neighborhood of the dead', and he took the road that lead from the hills of the *barrio* to the zone of the rich people, which one would only cross by mistake or to run an errand.

Those from the neighborhood up the hill, used to weave stories of how their lives would be if one day they would succeed in closing a big deal in order to transfer their little things to the neighborhood of the rich and to leave the very high hills, the perpetual puddles covering the blind alleys, the crooks trying to make a couple of bucks on someone else's account and the indiscriminate massacres that took away friends, girlfriends or relatives without

## Pilgrims of Death

caring whether it was Sunday or Ash Wednesday. In his neighborhood, death used to run barefoot to not frighten away its victims, it used to jump on top of anyone at any time. Death, that shameless and reddish prostitute, was the most singular sword of Damocles which could be felt by the people from the neighborhood up the hill.

To come down from the hills, but to remain forever living in the sacred plains of the rich, was the most recondite and precious dream of the poor, who had to strengthen their legs from going up the slopes to get to their homes.

Mauro used to think about all of this, while the road became less steep, the smells less fetid, but more plastic and unreal, and his motorcycle would go into the domains of a Disneyland of play-dough, and a zone of everyone, but in reality of just a handful, in a torrent sea of technical and effeminate Americanized dreams, because sometimes power and money lose their perspective, the frontier between what is real and the ephemeral, the virtual and the mystic color rose. Mauro used to see his city up on the hill in perspective and longed for the life down the hill. He didn't care that life there was an eternal fiction, a daily comedy; he longed to

# ✠ Pilgrims of Death

leave behind his real city of encrusted brick walls, with graffiti and anonymous poems.

He couldn't wait for the time to live without the need to caress a pistol or a shotgun before going to bed, because up the hill, very few could give themselves the pleasure of not having living nightmares, waiting for the least negligence – to make them reality – in front of their eyes, and blow off their brain in a second.

Sacred city, native city, but a city of no one; just like the one down the hill, but in its piece of land, day by day, one could contemplate the burning hell, trying to earn space in the lucid smile of the young men.

In the city that Mauro knew, the gifts from Santa Claus did not exist; nor the items with batteries, or the trips to the beach, or the private pools. Everything was a different reality from the one lived by the people from the city down the hill. It was as simple as that; up or down; you either were or you were not; you either belonged or were excluded; there was nothing in between.

# PILGRIMS OF DEATH

## TWO

So many times he had seen death near by, that his eyes had already lost their capacity to feel astonished. At the age of four, he was already floating from house to house. When he was born, his father disappeared from the face of the earth and he would've loved to have had the opportunity to meet him so that he himself could send him straight to the cemetery – feet first – but his mother took with her the name of the one who brought him to this world, when in a shooting, death carried her in its claws; he was only four years old. From that point forward, his aunts raffled him as if he were in a public auction and he grew up without knowing a true home, until at age thirteen he decided to flee from Aunt Gloria's house to go to the house of *El Cacique,* as they used to call him, a butcher that during his free time was a killer and a crack dealer.

At the age of eight, Mauro knew of *'sacol'*, hunger and loneliness. At ten, marihuana, crack; anything useful to travel away from a filthy world in order to land in a cloud of daydreams – unreal but brief – until he would return to feel the pain upon falling on that asphalt of reality.

At thirteen, he proved 'his cunning', when he stabbed –

# Pilgrims of Death

with a butcher's knife – a thief that pretended to steal from el Cacique, and it was there where they began to train him for bigger jobs. He started with simple jobs: to hold up unprepared old ladies who were coming out of church, to robbing drunks or assaulting street vendors. Then, he started doing more diverse jobs; from stealing shoes from a drunk to holding up supermarkets, and later on, he made the big jump when he was 'entrusted to eliminate someone'.

He was so scared, that he could not sleep that night thinking about what would happen if he got caught, but his nerves of steel didn't allow him to wait and his aim worked to his advantage at the moment he 'knocked out'– with one shot to the head – a mathematics teacher who had a reputation of corrupting and abusing the children from a school. He never knew who paid him because everything was done through el Cacique, but with the money from 'the job', he bought new sneakers and marihuana so that everyone in hell could smell it.

From that day forward, his fame of firm pulse and cold veins spread like malaria, and there was no job he turned away, nor was there any live man who didn't end up dead.

# Pilgrims of Death

He used to send to the other world anyone entrusted to him. He was a relaxed guy by nature, and almost always would react if he would feel he was being followed. He didn't kill for pleasure, only for necessity, or if the job given to him would demand it. But very soon, death for Mauro was a mockery of destiny or a candle to the Virgin, when it was a question of doing 'a job' so that the same Virgin would protect him and death would come for the other man, not him.

He began ascending quickly in the short and crooked scale of values that would allow his condition, and soon he positioned himself in a precious wage scale where he had to sleep with one eye open and not even believe in his own shadow. He was the leader of a gang, a thing that lasted for a very short time, because few days after beginning their runs as a group, all members were killed while robbing a bank. It was presumed that an informant ruined the party and the other partners died in the attempt – seven in total – and Mauro, the tough one, the loner, was left behind with a bullet on his left shoulder and with a craving for swallowing the whole city with its police force, prostitutes, its priests, its politicians, trash

# Pilgrims of Death

and anyone else at whatever time whichever way. He became so angry with the city, that when he had a chance he went to El Cacique to pick up his few belongings.

"I am leaving", he said, holding a tear that began to betray him.

"Where to?" asked the tutor.

"Wherever; right to hell, to the cemetery, what the hell matter where to; my friends were killed and I was the only one who escaped. Death must have something in mind since it didn't feel like taking me too," he said, putting in a bag a pair of pants and some stamps from the Virgin of Carmen.

"Don't talk nonsense, Mauro that if they didn't kill you is because you are the best", said the other man.

"Best of what, don't tell me that crap that I was the first one when the cops began shooting; all, all of them ended up on the floor and don't ask me how I escaped because I don't have the slightest idea as to how I got out of that bank alive. To me, that bitch called death, wanted to mock me and at this moment she must be laughing non-stop because I don't know what happened. I don't even remember how many cops I managed to kill, my mind went blank and I don't recall anything that happened after the first shot when *el Flaco* fell down by

## Pilgrims of Death

my side like a sack of dirty clothes ... What the hell man, what happened? I don't know, but starting today I'll never again hook up with gangs, all of them entrusted me and I failed them. Starting today I will do 'my work' alone; after all, I've always been alone", said Mauro at the door of the butcher shop.

"Stay, Mauro, chances are they might be looking for you," El Cacique said.

"Good; if they're looking for me tell them that I'll be over Diana's. I'll wait for them there; I'll wait for whomever and for whatever. But you, old Cacique, don't worry that I'll always have you in my heart and whatever pertains to you pertains to me. You are the father I never met and I owe you all I am …but I better leave now because if I start crying you're going to think that I am a wimp."

Mauro embraced the man who had given him protection during many years, and he felt he was going into a new and unknown world. The embrace was short, full of energy, almost abrupt, and he turned around before el Cacique could see his tears.

# Pilgrims of Death

He went as he had mentioned, over Diana's his great love; a tall brunette of dangerous curves where he learned the arts of love and infidelity. Diana was too much of a woman for one man, and Mauro, after murdering two of her seasonal lovers, gave up and decided not to continue to stain himself for the mulatta who made his life like a carrousel.

Diana had met him when he was only fifteen years old, and took him to her house after one of her lovers' burial, Andrés', and coincidentally one of Mauro's friends. They met for the first time at the cemetery, and the statuesque Diana took him to her house where she undressed him before he could say anything. From that moment forward their bodies remained intertwined in one embrace and the sporadic infidelities of Diana, fortified even more the character of the young man. It was precisely due to the fortress and warrior and noble character of the young man – and due to the infidelities of his Diana – that among his closest collaborators they called him El Toro behind closed doors.

It was there, at Diana's, where he learned about heroine, whisky and the refined liquors. There was no beer or cheap drinks, there he only consumed the best; from her body of a goddess to her cable channels.

When Diana found out about the bank and saw Mauro arrive with a plastic bag, she knew that their lives wouldn't be the same. And they were not; because Mauro's character and luck totally changed to the point that he had become an institution, a man respected and sought by the most prestigious mob groups.

The future began smiling to them; it was Mauro who had more than one lover and Diana the one who would get angry until she exploded. Destiny's tricks had come to her humble apartment, and now it was he who would establish the rules. With the turn of time, the stay of the young man over Diana's home became more sporadic, until he himself decided that the best thing to do was to cut ties in good terms by leaving the golden ass brunette so that she could live her own life.

He moved into a modest apartment where he lived alone, but always accompanied by women and a handful of friends. In his mind, always Diana; in his body, a thousand women but always Diana constantly present in

# ☥ Pilgrims of Death

multicolor, in sepia, high or sober; Diana with her breasts made of gold, her smile of goddess. Diana in the mornings, and she herself at night, in other bodies, it was always Diana. Not caring about age, or motives, it was always her, with her freckles, with her beauty mark in her sex and her wavy braids. Many skins, lots of blood and many deaths happened so that he could enjoy life without longing for the woman who taught him how to love.

He became an expert hunter. Some times hunted, sometimes lost but always triumphant, victorious and proud of his luck and aim.

"With this little job I'll buy me a car. Now I can get rid of this bike and dedicate myself to the good life", Mauro thought while a smell of fried chicken indicated to him that he had arrived at the shopping mall; he would be picked up there to be taken to his boss, because no matter how far he had come in his career, he had never been able to step over the barrier of the unreachable, to know for a fact where his boss could be found.

# PILGRIMS OF DEATH

Patiently, he focused on reviewing his appearance, so that his boss wouldn't see him with filthy shoes and he was glad to confirm that a lovely girl of voluminous breasts – with no hesitation – was daringly looking at him over the shoulder of a man who appeared to be her husband, corroborating that his look was acceptable.

"There's no problem; with 'this look,' I even pick up dead people", he thought.

He looked at his watch, and he affirmed that he was on time for the appointment. And willing to wait calmly, he sat at a bench in the park. Five minutes after having arrived, a black car of polarized glass slowly got closer.

Mauro recognized him right away and approached him calmly while the back door of the car opened. If he had imagined for an instant that the order he would receive was against everything he had accomplished until now, perhaps he would have never got on it.

# Pilgrims of Death

### THREE

An hour later, after unexpected turns, senseless stops, up and down hills, going and returning, absolute silence, a radio station with a bad reception about to explode his ear drums, a black bandage, that did not even allow a bad thought through his sight, a headache created by the sensation of entrapment, a double shot of *aguardiente* to relax him and let him be with his feet on the ground to face the boss. Finally, they took away the cloth that covered his sight and the light of a splendorous eternal spring afternoon hurt his hazel eyes.

The boss's boys were very courteous because they knew of Mauro's qualities and his cold blood, but they did not have any problem in tasting the triumph one gets from feeling superior in number and in category. They were all paid assassins that hardly knew how to read which didn't help because in order to shoot they were handed weapons without instructions. And since in order to kill a Decalogue has not ever been completely written, they could very well be illiterate or retired shysters, it didn't matter… As a matter of fact, what was indispensable was to learn not to see or to listen to nothing in absolute; nothing that would be beyond of what was allowed.

# Pilgrims of Death

Very few knew that that house had been the crib of an illustrious musician and for many years belonged to the municipality due to the bureaucratic process of a judicial dispute. Upon dying, the grandson of the musician in question, began the succession of the old big house, since the one that could have amended the mistake seemed content with the anguish of his descendants, and exhaled his last breath without leaving his last will recorded in sealed paper.

This was how the old mansion, direct descendant of Manorial houses of the colony – a thousand times restored and furnished with a costly Victorian style – had seen passed by her corridors laymen, monks, cops, pipe-fitters, beggars, orphans, rest facilities, asylums and a great number of more usages that would vary according to the taste or interests of the politicians in power. Until the strong arm of the boss, erased – by the stroke of the pen – the disputes and bought without rhyme or reason the squandered mansion.

The attorney who signed the sale of the house, and the one who appraised the transaction, were found inside potato bags in an abandoned region north side of the city with a single bullet-hole in the skull; a complete

# Pilgrims of Death

indifference by the police accompanied those assassinations.

It was a country house, in the heart of the city. It had thirteen ample bedrooms, four patios, two kitchens, a swimming pool, and a back yard full of mango trees. Besides, it had a huge basement where according to the oral traditions of the city, the biggest and never seen arsenal, and a cocaine processing laboratory were hidden. Legend or fiction, only a handful of people knew it.

At the main entrance one could see a sign that said: 'Welcome', devoured by the grass, and another more daring in neon lights, that stated: 'No trespassing'.

On both sides of the main entrance, with a metallic fence, armed vigilantes and German shepherds trained to bite even a sigh, were two palm trees of the most strange specie – twisting flirtatiously – to an insinuating staggering instigated by the lightest breeze.

It was there where Mauro was taken. The mansion was so well covered that despite being located in the heart of the

## Pilgrims of Death

city, its exuberant vegetation, its protected-colored mud walls and its retreat home style made it look like a convent of inoffensive monks, and not a dump of death.

"Wait here," said a bully that was walking in leather boots as if he were riding upon walking.
"And where do you think I'm going to go?" answered Mauro, sluggishly.

While sitting in a comfortable black leather sofa with white rhomboidal incrustations, he reviewed his sins just in case the boss would ask him for an account of his actions.

So many stories were woven about that house, that he shouldn't take things lightly. For instance, it was said that the backyard was not such, but that in less than five years it had become the biggest common grave of the city; that the spirits of the deceased wandered without rest along the corridors and they had even seen them swimming in the pool.

It was rumored that only those He respected he would execute them with his own hand, and the list of the fallen in those narrow passages was countless.

# Pilgrims of Death

"I am not 'a snake' of the Boss; it's been a long time that I only do what he orders me, and with exception of one or two deceased, I only 'knocked out' those he ordered me to, so, I don't have to be afraid," he thought.

The Boss had never treated him badly, and in multiple occasions in which he saw him, the meetings were always cordial; business appointments where there was room for jokes, but mostly for serious issues such as kidnappings or executions.

Mauro was part of the armed branch which the Boss enjoyed calling 'my angels of justice.' There was never talk of murders, or massacres, or vengeance; they were simply and fully considered 'celestial justice.' And the celestial did not stop only by its name: it was something more mystic, more purified and refined. It was the blue death. In the scene of the crime they always left a piece of celestial color clothing, at times only a light blue tone ribbon; their executions left an indelible mark of their journey without prejudice for the life of others, to exchange their last black sorrow, black death, black silence, black emptiness by the blue sky, of a hope that was only knotted in the perverted mind of the one who plotted all, was capable of all and would pay all… the Boss.

Thanks to Mauro's broad experience, he was given a membership to the 'angels of justice' as a voiceless member of the group. He never acted with someone, they never made him go in the group and he did not have a supervisor who wasn't the Boss himself or the boss's brother.

Mauro was dying of thirst but he knew that in that house one did not ask for anything; there, one waited with patience, submission and obedience until the voice of the strong man would make itself noticed, not before. But after, one should not request anything either because in that house and in that city, only what the Boss wished for was done.

# ℡ Pilgrims of Death

### FOUR

A giant clock adorned the bedroom; its metallic warriors were ready to throw the bells into the air in their wooden cedar coffer. The eccentricities of the Boss were already legendary, but his taste for antiques was even more. The rumor was that he had paid over a million dollars for a sword it was said to have belonged to Napoleon, but not only did he take an interest in the past, his classic pleasures varied like the tropical climate. At times, he would buy the latest convertible model or a piece from a museum of more than five hundred years of age, other times, he simply enjoyed investing his money in fragments of a papyrus with more than three thousand years of history, or simple chairs and furniture of colonial times.

When he was in a good mood, he could pay a sum no matter how much, for a parchment, a nail, an arch, a suit or a mommy as long as he was guaranteed that it was a real antique. For that he used to consult with *el Bizco*, his right hand in art matters; a real living encyclopedia. It was precisely him who discovered the deceiver who dared to swindle the Boss with an original Michael Angelo. When el Bizco found out that it was a despicable copy, he told the Boss and the latter, courteously, and

# PILGRIMS OF DEATH

without losing his disposition extended his hand to the seller, he grabbed it with force, like someone who closes a deal, and he cut it off completely with a sword from his collection. The hand of the supposedly salesman remained hanging in a red sea, and the rest of his body was never found.

This is how the boss was; a gentleman of medieval costumes, indigenous malice, manners for any occasion, and an enormous greed. No one knew exactly how old he was, but his joviality and strength made him look less old than he was.

Nobody knew his real name either, since everyone would vow to him with the only one they knew: Boss; that was it. Not even his most intimate friends, or his girlfriends dared to call him differently. It was one of the things that united him the most with Mauro, the enigmatic way in which life had labeled them.

The Boss had thousands of collection items in the most recondite places of the country and abroad, in which the following were included: whales, queens, politicians, weapons, antiques, zoos, relics, medieval castles, cars,

# Pilgrims of Death

yachts and even a space ship which nobody ever knew whether it worked or not. The majority of the thirteen bedrooms of the great house were simple warehouses of the most diverse and costly species.

He was married once with the only woman who, according to him, he had loved in his life, until an encephalic cancer consumed her and snatched her from him before he could take her to Canada for treatment.

From that moment on, he became more reserved with women, but there were many who passed by his bedrooms; from models, beauty queens, ministers, athletes or secretaries. He would conquer the one he craved for with a pearl, a car, a horse or a serenade; none could resist the overwhelming charm of the most powerful man in the country.

He not only was attractive for his countless possessions and fortune, within the country and abroad, he was also a seductive man with strong complexion, tall and romantic. His black hair made a contrast with his brown eyes and his dark skin. He possessed a well built body, thanks to the care that he gave himself, in his personal

# Pilgrims of Death

gymnasium, or with the sports that he practiced outside when the security conditions would allow it.

He loved mountain climbing, but when you are the most wanted man in the country it is difficult to go out to practice said sport, therefore, he ordered to build, inside one of his buildings, an artificial wall to climb. Swimming and karate presented less risk and were among his favorite practices.

But what the Boss appreciated the most were his two children: Viviana and José, born of his only wife, his greatest love.

# ⚜ Pilgrims of Death

### FIVE

Viviana, the youngest, was his spoiled child. He had ordered to bring a babysitter from Switzerland and a private instructress from France who was to be in charge of her education. Although she was only fourteen, she spoke perfect English, French and Italian; she read works of Dostoyeski in Russian, she recited poems by Rimbaud and sang opera with a strong soprano voice.

When Vivy, as he used to call her, turned seven, he ordered to build a scaled replica of the Disney Fantasy palace in one of his haciendas, with such precision that those who saw it became ecstatic due to the architectonic beauty of the construction, and the accurate details and colors, hence when it came to taste, the Boss did not hesitate to spend his money.

Nothing and no one was an obstacle, and money was not an object when the whims of the girl were made known. It did not matter what it was, as long as she fulfilled her private school duties.

Once during Christmas, the French instructress, of iron character and exquisite culture, let the Boss know that the girl was not fulfilling her duties selflessly and the father told her:

# Pilgrims of Death

"Prepare a test and do it in the room of the mirrors. If my daughter does not respond correctly, be sure that I will punish her exemplarily, but if she responds perfectly to the entire questionnaire, you can say goodbye to your job and your life, because I myself will make you eat your words for having put in doubt Vivy's abilities."

The room of the mirrors was a rectangular room, in one of the Boss's country side properties which had mirrors and ivory encrustations in all the walls but behind them there were no walls but video cameras and an adjacent living room where he could spy any way he wanted to whomever he wanted.

The instructress gave her an oral and a written test, and that day the results were disastrous. The Boss did not say a word. He called his daughter and took her to a stable. He opened the door and showed her a dozen ponies of the most diverse colors.

"This was your Christmas present", he told her. "They are ponies imported from Corsica. They were for you. But for sure today they will leave this house without

# ⁂ Pilgrims of Death

you having enjoyed them for one second because mediocrity is not allowed here. If you study, you will get what you deserve and whatever you wish for, because you are my princess, but if you do the contrary, in the same way you will get what you deserve."

The same day the father sent the dozen horses to another location and he was not moved by the crystal drop of dew sliding on Viviana's Face. As far as she was concerned, she never made more scenes, because she very well knew that in front of his dad they were worthless. He was able to do whatever was necessary for her, but he put his strict character before any scrupulous. Resignedly, that's how she swallowed her pride and dedicated herself to studying like her father wanted.

The relationship that Vivy had with his brother was so tight that they seemed to possess telepathy powers. Whatever was done to one of them, the other would enjoy it or would suffer it. Him; Jose, the oldest son, was the reason that Mauro was waiting in the antechamber.

# PILGRIMS OF DEATH

## SIX

With nerves of bronze, Mauro waited for his Boss to show up, and he was quite impressed when one of the bullies arrived dressed with a suit of a perpetual burier.

"Come with me, He wants to talk to you downstairs," he said.
"Downstairs?" His voice was not able to hide a slight sense of fear. "Are you sure he said downstairs?"

"Yeah man, are you deaf or what?, downstairs. Don't worry that we already tied up the dragons… Don't tell me that you also believe in the stupid things they say about this house"… said the bully bursting out in laughter and Mauro was forced to second it, but without conviction.

While he walked through luxurious corridors filled with Persian tapestry, Mauro dried the sweat provoked by his nerves.

"*Downstairs?*" He wandered, "*but if they say that nobody 'goes in' downstairs. And what if he plans to do is to shoot me down there? Well, what the heck, I'm already here and there's no turning back.*"

# Pilgrims of Death

He was lead through an intricate labyrinth of stairs and passages. The beauty of the objects of the house he had only seen on TV. The yards and more yards of imported fabrics, covering doors and narrow passages; the pricy vases, the armory, helmets, swords, weapons and chairs; everything made a beautiful contrast of fascinating colors, that soon the young man forgot his worries and delightfully enjoyed the rare panorama being introduced to his eyes.

He never knew how many narrow passages he must have walked or how many doors he went through in order to get to one made of oak, with a single golden lion in one side and two bullies on the other. The men looked at him calmly and greeted him with a familiar nodding of the head, without saying a word.

Death waited for him on the other side, he knew that for sure; not being so, they would not have allowed him to see what – from a distance – was perceived as the private office of the great Boss. All the men looked at each other waiting for something that Mauro couldn't decipher. They remained calm and he was the only one who felt the perspiration on his new shirt.

# PILGRIMS OF DEATH

A couple of minutes, perpetual like a farewell, and cold as indifference came over the waiting room, while the staring of the feline statue scrutinized him incessantly.

Without notice, the oak door opened and the body guard that had escorted him there invited him to come in with a dry and arrogant smile.

Mauro went in the dwelling and felt the door close behind them. Before him, there was an ample carpeted living room, full of collectable weapons; cross-bows, swords, daggers, arches, arrows, knives and even rocks. All seemed so old, that it could not be considered a warlike armory; it looked more like a collection of outdated artifacts. Upon observing around the room, Mauro could not contain his smile upon thinking that the whole city was shaking worrying about a enormous arsenal, when in reality what was hidden there were formidable museum pieces, without any danger to society.

In front of a fictitious colossal fireplace, logs were burning without consuming, thanks to the kindness of electricity. Next to it, there was a rustic desk, without any decoration except a paper-knife, two self-portraits and a newspaper.

# Pilgrims of Death

In front of the empty chair, one could appreciate the oil painting of a young and beautiful face of a boy of about fifteen years of age, lightened by a reflector that made his smile illuminate the entire room.

Before Mauro could come out of his stupor of finding himself in a warrior museum, a voice called him from a side of the fireplace; the person that spoke to him was contemplating the painting backwards from the door.

"It's beautiful, don't you think?" said the voice with a nostalgic tone.
"Good afternoon, Boss," the one that was asked dared to say.
"Don't you think?" replied the immutable voice.
"Yes, it is, it's beautiful Boss", Mauro responded.
"It is", said the voice, while turning to be face-to-face with him.

The boss had an unusual aspect in him. The people that knew him knew that he was someone luxuriant, austere and jovial. The one in front of Mauro had blackish circles under his eyes, a lost stare and a sad expression on his face.

# Pilgrims of Death

The man walked towards Mauro with a serene and firm pace, with his stare always lost in the pupils of the paid assassin. He extended his hand and grabbed it with a strong grip, almost with ire, while he invited him to continue to look at the painting.

"Thanks for coming brother" said the Boss's voice and a stream of hot blood bathed the body of the young man, because although He had always treated him with respect, it was the first time that He treated him this way.

*"Now, it's time for me to say good bye; I'm fried. The only thing left is for him to shoot me after that really strange welcome"*, thought the young man.

But contrary to what he was expecting, he was served a double shot of whisky and was invited to sit down next to the fireplace next to the Boss. There were no more stiffed meetings or to-be-on-the-look-out bodyguards, because the Boss had ordered the bully that accompanied them to leave the room.

Mauro was sipping his drink calmly, and little by little had managed to recuperate his common tranquility.

# Pilgrims of Death

The Boss invited him again to look at the exposed over-the-wall painting, came close to it and got lost in a deep waive of contemplation.

"Isn't true that is lovely?" he asked.

"Yes, Boss; but with all due respect, don't ask me who did it because I don't know anything about those things", answered the young man.

"I'm not asking you about the painting, I'm asking you about the face. Do you know who he is?" asked the owner of the house without a rush.

Mauro swallowed saliva. He tried to remember if he had ever seen in any place those features but the face, as much as it seemed familiar, didn't bring absolutely anything to his memory.

He forced himself to remember – in case his life would depend on this answer – but nothing came to mind.

"You have to excuse me Boss, but I don't know who the boy is. But if you want, I'll find out", answered Mauro diligently.

## PILGRIMS OF DEATH

The Boss took his stare away from the painting and placed it like an arrow upon his colloquist, but with no anger; with a glassy and profound look he told him:

"The one you're looking at is my son. It's because of him that I have called you."

# ✠ Pilgrims of Death

### SEVEN

Mauro knew of the profound love that the Boss had for his two children, but it had been a long time since anyone had seen them in the city. The rumor was that they were staying in a farm near the Amazonas; others said that they were in the shore and others would affirm that they had taken refuge in Germany or in Miami.

There was such an array of misinformation about the Boss's children that they could have very well been drinking coffee in the middle of the city, few blocks away from that house, and nobody knew of their whereabouts. Well, this is what Mauro believed and like him, most of the people.

"Do you know my son?" asked the man.

"I met him two years ago when you had the party in the Bull-fighting arena" answered Mauro choosing carefully his words.

"You have good memory."

"Thank you, Boss."

"There's a reason why you are one of the best."

"Thank you, Boss."

"Tell me something Mauro, do you have children?"

"Not that I know Boss."

"So, you don't know what is to feel that you can give your life for your child, for the blood of your blood."

"Well, I'd give my life for you Boss. You know that whatever concerns you, concerns me."

"Thanks boy but I'm not talking about that. You say that you would give your life for me because I'm the one who pays you and because if you fail you would pay me back, as simple as that."

Mauro was musing on the glass of whisky and the pieces of ice formed strange signals of distress, while they submerged themselves in the liquor, dancing by the rhythm of his shaking hand. He did not know what to answer because what he had just heard was the simple truth.

"Don't act like that Mauro that with that paleness you're going to end up spilling your drink on your shirt; is it new?"

"Pardon me?"

"Is it new?"

"New? The painting?"

"No man, your shirt; is it new?"

# Pilgrims of Death

Mauro had no other choice but to blush and agree with his head while the Boss indicated to get close to the painting.

"Is pretty, isn't it?"

"Well, yes, I liked it a lot and I bought it for me today" answered Mauro triumphantly.

"I'm talking about his face" the Boss pointed to the painting and Mauro became pale again.

"Ah, forgive me Boss; yes, he has a pretty face."

"It's a great painting; it reflects the intensity and the beauty of my son."

"Yes, Boss."

"Do you know why I ordered to call you?"

"Well, I don't know… But for whatever it is, count on me."

"'Whatever it is' is a huge statement boy, I could ask you whatever and you would be obligated, for the simple fact of having pronounced those words."

"It's the truth Boss. I have a lot to be grateful for to you and your brother. If it hadn't been for your help of you both who knows what would I have become of me now," Mauro said with an almost mystic devotion.

# Pilgrims of Death

"Thank you for your loyalty Mauro, but don't look at me as if I were God because I am a simple mortal, a mortal with the soul destroyed."

"Don't say one more word, Boss. Tell me who destroyed it and I will destroy who destroyed it" Mauro solemnly replied emphasizing his words in a theatrical manner.

"Man, Mauro, you really are a character. This is probably why I like to commend you to the most difficult task."

"For whatever, Boss."

"How long have you not heard anything about my son?"

"Wow, Boss, you put me in a difficult spot because there's no much talk in the city about him or your family."

"Don't talk nonsense Mauro that we well know that all the time they are making up a new story."

"Well, the last news that I heard was that they were in the United States but that was many months ago.

"I'm going to tell you a little bit about my son, the rest, you're going to find out for me." The Boss

# ❧ Pilgrims of Death

remained staring at the painting for a long time and when he invited Mauro to sit down again the ice cubes had already melted in his empty glass.

The Boss walked to an oak barrel, and made spin a silver knife, upon doing it the upper portion of the barrel opened and uncovered some bottles of liquor. He took the whisky one and filled Mauro's glass to the top. The latter made a sign of not wanting more, but the Boss told him:

"Drink it slowly; I assure you that when you hear the task that I'm going to give you, you're going to need a double shot."

Mauro noticed that the Boss put the bottle on the desk, not before pouring himself a drink. Sitting there, he could observe the barrel behind the Boss's back and the painting on his right. A thread of cold sweat bathed the young man's new shirt. Nor the armory, nor the spectacular weapons, nor the painting, not even the whisky, were able to call so much his attention, as the tremendous curiosity of knowing why he was sitting there conversing with the most powerful man in the country.

"How long is it that you know my brother Oscar?" asked the Boss abruptly taking Mauro out of his pondering.

"Hmm, much longer than I know you… Yes, I met him like a year before I met you. He was precisely the one who introduced me to you."

"How long ago?"

"About five years ago, Boss."

"That's a long time, right?"
The Boss paused and then he added:

"And, you like my brother?"

"What a question Boss, if I respect both of you like the family I never had" answered Mauro sweating profusely.

"I'm not talking about me: I'm asking about my brother Oscar."

"I appreciate him a lot. Oscar is the only one I don't call 'Don'; he is like a godfather to me; the one who gave me one of the most interesting jobs, he took me out of that muddy place and helped me get into your organization. I owe your brother meeting you and I have a great friendship with him," answered Mauro trying to prevent the knot in his throat not to betray him.

# Pilgrims of Death

"How long have you not seen my brother?"
"I saw him about a month ago."
"Where"?
"In the airport, I went with him because he was going on vacation to the beach with a girl. That Oscar is good people, yes or no?"

For every answer, the Boss filled his glass and galloped it up at once. He filled his glass again, looked at the smiley face in the painting one more time and turned himself around until he was face to face with Mauro. He remained standing with his stare penetrating the thoughts of the young man, he left his glass on the desk and continued to scrutinize the – each time more anxious – look of the boy whom he had ordered to call.

"My son Jose is one of the things that I love the most in this world, and a month ago he was killed" said the Boss, without a tremor in his throat.

Mauro was astonished. He was so afraid that he didn't realize that he was pouring his drink on his new shirt. He didn't know whether he had heard correctly or if the drink had gone to his head.

# Pilgrims of Death

"I cannot return Jose to life. This pain goes beyond any other I have ever received and I think that I will never recover from this loss."

There was an uncomfortable silence, one of those sticky one that penetrate your bones and go to your respiratory system and when you least expect it, is resounding through your brain. That's the way that silence was; tense, frigid and direct, like the words of the Boss when he passed judgment.

"I ordered to bring you to ask you for a favor."
"Boss, I don't know how to say 'I'm sorry' but believe me that I'm hurt by the loss and I am here for whatever."
"I want you to find and kill my brother Oscar."

## ⚜ Pilgrims of Death

### EIGHT

The night that the Boss saw his son for the last time, he embraced him vigorously and told him to take care of himself, explaining to him that it was better for him to 'disappear' for a few days and take refuge in one of his most remote haciendas. He gave his brother Oscar the assignment of transferring and protecting Jose. He trusted blindly the ability of his most important deputy. It was he, his younger brother who was always willing to use his contacts, persistence to standout, by finding easy money to serve his powerful brother; therefore, he was the most important player in the security interlocking of his organization.

The operation to have Jose transported to the Boss's recreational farm in the valleys 600 kilometers near the capital, was only a simulation, because where they really transported him was to *Las Lomas*, one of the Boss's rural houses where he used to hide once in a while. It was a place near the city, with easy access to the roads and a small tunnel intentionally built, from the kitchen of the house to an alternate route, ever forgotten by the hand of God and man.

# Pilgrims of Death

Oscar was a corpulent, athletic and attractive man, with a reputation of being a womanizer and heavy drinker that would go beyond the limits of reality. It was said that he had more women than Salomon and that he had never gotten married because he did not want to give anyone the luxury of bothering his life. His *Don Juan* impulses made him commit the worse absurdities and the most eccentric waste of money that the city would have never been informed.

If he wanted a woman, he had no inconvenience nor scrupulous to conquer her which ever way fit him. There were stories of men he had ordered to execute, only for the pleasure of being alone with their women for one weekend; that was sufficient for him; thereafter they were a package that he would never assume to own.

If he courted the woman of any of his men, he would send them far away, in remote and unlikely missions, while he besieged the chosen lady with gifts and serenades…until he succeeded his wish, and almost all would fall under his pressure, whether for desire, interest, or fear of repercussions due to his unlimited power.

# Pilgrims of Death

When the Boss said good bye to his son, he approached the pickup truck where Oscar was giving orders on the radio and told him:

"I trust you with his life, you know that this is becoming difficult and we need to be very cautious. I have put up with many of your mistakes, so be extra careful. You are accountable for him!"

"As always, don't worry," Oscar answered, giving the signal to begin the maneuvers to transport his nephew.

Under normal circumstances, he would have simply taken a helicopter and they would have taken Jose without more preambles. But about a week before, the other mafia group in the city had declared open war against his family and properties. The latter, due to Oscar's miscalculated plans of attack, which instead of placing a car bomb in the installations of a building where the sporting cars collection of the security chief of the mafia of the north of the country was, due to misinformation, he instead blew up in pieces the building where the aunt and sister of the second most powerful man of the organized mafia lived.

## Pilgrims of Death

The reaction, upon knowing the death of his relatives did not take long, and a violent slaughter between the two mafias began, breaking the cold war that had kept them together for several months.

The country was managed by two omnipotent mafia groups that would shake the foundations of political, union, religious and industrial sectors that were so prestigious and exclusive. No one escaped the macabre and slippery hand of the mafia.

It was due to this, that when the war between the two groups erupted, the constant river of innocent blood did not take long to begin. Age, position, money did not matter anymore; the only thing that mattered was to mark the territory with as many dead bodies as possible. This is how the modality of the planned massacres through *car-bombs* was born, because the need to be noticed was so imperious that paid assassins were used in special cases, but the massacres, the real life transgressions, those that made noise upon making a shopping mall, a building or a town disappear were the most effective methods in matters of death. Any insurgent group was well seen by the mafia leaders,

## Pilgrims of Death

since those groups would serve indistinctively any master, not caring about his beliefs; the only thing they needed was the payment for the honoraries and they would take care to dynamite an entire town before dawn; all disguised under the scheme of democracy.

The cities slept in tranquility, families were afraid and no one escaped the deadly whip of the mafia and its madness for power. A bomb could explode on a street, on a flying plane, a store, school, police station, it was all the same. For the bosses of the cartels, what mattered was to be watchful and standing strong on their ground, to scare away and intimidate their adversaries. Due to the bomb that Oscar ordered to place in the city of his adversaries, the game of cards unchained tumbling down. The supposed peace and the nonverbal agreement of no aggression between adversary groups were so fragile that any excuse to detonate the conflict between the bosses of the mafia would have been perfect. The only difference was that in the attempt, direct relatives of the other group were killed which made it a concrete reason. Then, the order was clear: death to the whole family of the Boss.

## Pilgrims of Death

This is how the biggest slaughter started, the merciless war, where it did not matter if a school blew up in pieces, the least and most fragile information that would indicate that a relative of the Boss was in a shopping mall was the only thing needed to blow it up along with its surroundings; if afterwards they would realize that it was a false alarm, it was no cause of concern for they would find someone to blame; the country always had the *Guiney pigs* for that. One would resort to the lies of rigor, to the escapes of gas, to the subversive attempts; there was always a way to cover up the miscalculated errors of the mafia and their death machinery.

The Boss never imagined that the life and the security of his relatives were so vulnerable.

# PILGRIMS OF DEATH

## NINE

The young man's escort arrived to Las Lomas; once there, it started a forced but normal retreat for Jose; he was used to that type of absences of reality.

Jose, the hope of his father, his pride and his soul, never characterized himself for being bad-intentioned or inured to anything. He possessed a peaceful impenetrable demeanor and a refined culture that was the joy of his father.

He was never trained in the concerning matters of the drug trafficking business and although Jose knew where such power and wealth came from, he never showed interest in knowing the operation of his father's organization; he only dreamed of traveling peacefully around the world with his sister, and to see the architectural wonders that the orb was keeping for him.

They arrived at nightfall, and the little house, decorated with exquisite taste, boasted its beauty, even through the ragged geography and by the tangled vegetation that tried to camouflage it. The house was located in a small hill wherefrom one could see an

## Pilgrims of Death

entire valley cultivated with coffee; it was white with an impeccable ivory, and its red tile roof was plagued with a savage moss that seemed to be planted on purpose to protect it and hide it from interfering eyes.

Oscar went to check on the security systems to make sure they were functioning properly, while Jose calmly went to the main living room, to watch TV; he was well aware that he was not allowed to participate in those activities which he didn't really care about. The video cameras were hiding within the bi-floras and ferns that were hanging from the ceiling; a sophisticated system of infrared lights detected any unexpected visitor from the corridors to the windows; they had acquired that mechanism, along with a shipment of weapons, purchased from a Lebanese mercenary, specialized in supplying to the wars wherever they were happening, or in instigating them where they did not exist.

In addition to the high technology that the house had, they also disposed of a more domestic protection system; trained dogs ran through the surroundings of the house and nobody in his right mind would ever dare to confront those teeth ready to gore into the first person who would interfere; along with them, there

# ✠ Pilgrims of Death

were the bullies that always guarded the steps of the young boy.

Jose's life had become, despite of his grief, such a tight string of security that he could not walk to any place that he wanted to, but only to where he was directed to; his escorts protected him more than a rock star.

After making sure that the monitors' devices – hidden in a tiny room near the living room on the first floor – was working, and after communicating with his brother to inform him that the first phase of the mission was completed, Oscar went to the living room and stayed with Jose a long while, in which they shared, made jokes and drank hot chocolate prepared by Anselmo, the farm's superintendent, who was always willing to serve his bosses.

"I think we'd better go to sleep now," said Oscar, distant.

"How long is it going to be this time, uncle?"

"I don't know; but something tells met that the issue is more complicated now," replied Oscar.

"Why don't they also bring Vivy? I would like for us to be together," said Jose, with sorrow.

# Pilgrims of Death

"No, that is not a good idea for now. The best is that you not be together, thus having more opportunities to be unnoticed," tenderly answered the uncle.

Oscar followed Jose to the second floor bedroom, closed the curtains and vigorously hugged his nephew while he said good bye. He closed the door and he directed himself to the adjacent bedroom, where he always slept when he guarded someone from the family.

At the same time, the two bedrooms were surrounded by other rooms where six bodyguards slept, who were the relief of those who guarded the surroundings of the house. Nobody knew for sure if the enemy could trespass unnoticed through the information systems.

# Pilgrims of Death

## TEN

When Mauro woke up in the neighborhood's discotheque, he had spent three days without sleeping on a bed. After the Boss' ultimatum ordering him to kill Oscar, he had devoted himself to drinking, as if by drinking he could forget the heavy cross assigned to him.

Mauro crossed the security controls of the Boss's old mansion-museum as in a trance. After he was given his mission, he fell in a kind of hypnotic state; he was not able to say anything coherent and babbled like a baby. The Boss led him to the door of the studio and tapping his back, he corroborated:
"It's hard but it must be done… as simple as that."

Mauro went out through the door he had come in, but at the time, he no longer paid attention to the decorations, or the armory; he was amazed with a sea of doubts that lifted him off the earth and he didn't even know how he arrived in his motorcycle to the neighborhood, or at what time he had entered the discotheque.

That was the only place that understood the sorrows of the assassins and the young men who were about to have a hit and the meeting place to celebrate the happening. Around the discotheque, blood of all types had been spilled, but it was always open unconditionally for those that needed it. It was there that Mauro dropped himself on a chair and automatically began to drink non-stop. The owner of the place already knew him and although she was closing the establishment, she did not allow forcing out those who had the need to remain in and Mauro, whatever he was, had to be going through a tremendous internal search.  In reality, that was so; he had been assigned to kill his godfather, the only person he respected, feared and loved, after the Boss, of course.

It was Oscar who hired him for something really big, and from there, they became friends, despite the obvious differences between the two. When Mauro was making a name for himself, willingly, by tenacity, cold blood and good aim, Diana, his perpetual girlfriend, invited him to a celebration, where only the *'tough ones'* would attend, according to her explanation. In the party taking place in a farm near the city, Oscar approached Mauro and daggered his iron-like stare upon him by saying:

"So, you are the famous Mauro… a pleasure man, one can see you have toughness."

"Toughness, for what?" replied Mauro

# ✠ Pilgrims of Death

defensively.

At that moment, Diana went by and celebrated the fact that the two had already met, and without knowing that Mauro didn't know who that man with an athlete's physique was, introduced them in a second while going to the kitchen to get more grilled meat.

"Oscar?" Pardon me; are you Don Oscar the Boss's brother?"
"That's what they say but close your eyes boy that they are going to pop out," said Oscar with a friendly smile inviting Mauro to rush a shot of whisky.

Since that conversation, a great friendship began between the two; an implicit pact was closed between two worlds: the one from uphill, the one from the poor neighborhood that was in reality the one from downhill, and the one downhill – that of the powerful rich – which definitely was the one from uphill.

In that conversation, Mauro had his first taste of fire. Oscar entrusted him with the killing of a minister, and Mauro accepted the challenge; he felt that he was giving him the possibility to play in the major leagues. His life of waiting to be hired for small jobs to eliminate guys from the underworld, cops, or union leaders would be left behind; from that contract he could show that he was really worthwhile to an organization such as that of the Boss.

The days went by, and Mauro showed with his first *small job*, that he had come to stay under Oscar's orders. He knew that above him was his brother, but he admired and respected Oscar equally, for his boldness to plan and execute the riskiest plans.

Mauro became Oscar's right hand for a long time; no longer was there social limitations between them; they treated each other shoulder to shoulder. The Boss's brother used to take him to parties and trips across the country, searching for exotic women or risky businesses, it made no difference. Mauro, pleased, let himself – each time be taken higher in the organization and downward in his life.

They became each others' shadow. They killed together, got high together and never fought for a woman because for that Oscar made up the rules and Mauro followed

# ✠ Pilgrims of Death

them. Women were the only issue where Oscar did not allow himself to get into vain democracies; it was he who chose his lovers and Mauro who waited for the leftovers. The parties and feast of Bacchus lead by them would scandalize even the most liberal, but they never forgot a deal or let a shipment unprotected for the women; in that aspect, they were perfect professionals.

Once, after Mauro sent to 'the other world,' an army general, by a straight shot to the heart, he had to hide for a couple of months, and he did it under the watchful eye and care of Oscar, who facilitated everything for his hiding in one of the Boss's properties. There were so many things that Mauro had learned with that man that little was left to consider him his father, although there was only a ten- year difference between them. He had learned to love him as his own blood and because of it he was hurting in his stomach, head and soul by knowing that he had been ordered to kill him.

One afternoon, in his third day of drunkenness, two of the Boss's sicarios arrived at the discotheque, sat at the table with him and looked at him for a long time with pity and curiosity. One of them, the youngest one, placed his hand on his shoulder while telling him:

# Pilgrims of Death

"He's becoming impatient."

"Who"?

"Don't play dumb Mauro. You know that I'm talking about the Boss. He told us to tell you that enough with the drunkenness and to do what he entrusted you with or he will find someone else who will do the two jobs."

"What two jobs? I was only entrusted with one," replied Mauro.

"I don't know who you were ordered to kill but if you don't do it, he will find someone that will do it for you and then it will be your turn."

The man spoke with the same tone of voice, so calm, as if in a conversation among friends and although Mauro was not affected by the theme of death as if they were chatting about a soccer game as he was used to, this did not stop him from becoming pale, and his drunkenness dissipated before the eminence of confronting the reality he had been entrusted with.

"Tell the Boss not to worry; I will take care of it," he said at last, with confidence and a courage that was far

# ⚜ Pilgrims of Death

away from him to feel.

The men left the discotheque, and Mercedes, the owner of the place, worried, approached the boy.
"Whatever it was they asked you to do, be very careful Mauro, you don't play with those people."
"Ay, *Merceditas*, I already forgot what it is to play; I would give whatever so that this thing that I feel inside would be only a game… my heart is burning."

"If it hurts you so much, why don't you escape? Flee from the city; your soul is coming out your mouth and you are not like that."

Mauro kept looking at her, and for a second he imagined his godfather dead and him bathed in his blood. A timid tear ran down the young man's cheek and Mercedes saw him clean it. She got closer, ran her hand through his hair and then put away the glasses from the table and carried them cautiously to the counter. Upon returning to Mauro she told him:
"If it cannot be done any other way, do as you were told, or let your heart speak but don't torment yourself any more."

# PILGRIMS OF DEATH

Mauro did not leave without paying first and kissing the old lady Mercedes, in the cheek. The afternoon sun blinded his eyes, after being immersed in the darkness for so long.

Once again, he imagined being in front of his godfather, like in a stage where a tragic comedy was taken place: the tragic part of the plot was death; the comedy, the irony of life. The sicario and his friend were the actors. Mauro placed a pistol on his godfather's chest, and the other one did the same on Mauro's chest. After a signal, one could hear a hoarse sound and the smoke covered it all. The two of them looked at each other in silence with an accomplice smile in their lips; they were leaving this world as friends, as gentlemen, without betraying their eternal friendship. Then, the lights of the stage went off and the play ended with a thread of blood that dauntlessly ran through the floor.

Mauro woke up of that nightmare, just in time to jump a small print of blood on the street, without victims or injured people; that viscous material was more common than the water in his neighborhood.

He headed toward the altar of the virgin that was placed

# Pilgrims of Death

in the corner of the plaza. He got to it with devotion, and observed the candles that illuminated her image; it was the must-go place of every sicario. They went there with faith to ask for protection and aim; before any 'small job,' one needed to pray to be lucky to come out alive and to take away the life from the one they were responsible to. Mauro kept looking directly at the image and he could not find any reasons to take away the life of his godfather, friend and protector.

"What did I get myself into?" He reproached to himself, while he talked to the image, who in return gave him a porcelain smile.

He did not remember how much time he had spent longing for the good moments with Oscar, but when he recovered the notion of time, by his side, in front of the virgin's image, there was a man of a small stature, drunk and soaked in tears, who was observing the sculpture without paying attention to Mauro's presence. The drunkard placed a candle in the small altar and whispered:
"Let it be what is meant to be."
"The man departed from the monument, and Mauro kept thinking in the words that he had just heard. *Let it be what is meant to be,*" he thought, and he walked away with the image of the smiley statue on his back.

# PILGRIMS OF DEATH

## ELEVEN

The day that Jose was assassinated, his uncle Oscar felt that his life was ending. He would've wished the earth would've swallowed him, because if this happened it was only his fault.

After a long month hiding in Las Lomas, Oscar was becoming more and more bored and nervous. The days would go by and the spirit of war seemed to have calmed down; there were no more rumors of retaliation coming from his enemies, and when he made sure that things were so calmed, he decided to take a quick trip with a girlfriend to the country's seashore to relax and forget for a weekend the problems and the stress produced by guarding his nephew.

In the meantime, Jose entertained himself by reading and watching cable TV; he was not a boy who would allow to be intimidated by the sensation of reclusion, and although he missed his sister and his father, he tried to take things lightly, as if that time of retreat were a fieldtrip.

A sunny Thursday, Oscar called Mauro to take him to the airport. He could not afford the risk of going there

## ⚜ Pilgrims of Death

with several of his bodyguards, so he opted to call the closest and most abnegated one of his sicarios. He asked him to meet in the gas station near the trains and without further due, he hung up the phone. He looked for relief for his bullies, and he ordered to bring another set of bodyguards; he ordered them to be alert and on guard of his nephew, since he had to attend other important business that weekend.

He said farewell to Jose without major explanations, giving him a big hug and messing up his hair tenderly. He climbed his station wagon and left the farm alone. He had the precaution of not communicating his trip to his brother since he knew he would disapprove of that untimely escape which left his son much more vulnerable.

In the agreed place, he met with Mauro and after a couple of trivial comments they directed themselves to look for the woman that would accompany Oscar, a lavish green-eyed blonde with a black reputation.

Mauro never knew where his godfather was coming from, nor did he know why he had been so mysterious those days. On the other hand, Oscar never mentioned anything about his nephew, since the least his friend knew, it would be best for everyone.

This is how Mauro saw Oscar: tired and anxious to frisk with the astounding woman. He left them in the airport and returned in the station wagon, without asking any kind of questions; he was already accustomed to the pleasure trips of his godfather.

Oscar, hanging on his blonde's ass, boarded a plane that would take him to enjoy an unforgettable weekend, where liquor, drugs, and sex would be his inducement to forget the worries; nothing more distant from his reality since at the time that he was enjoying the pleasure of the sun and the sea, his cellular rang, taking away forever his smile, upon hearing the desperate voice of one of his lieutenants.
"Don Oscar, they killed us your nephew."

## TWELVE

Mauro, with his sorrow on his back, walked away from the image of the virgin, repeating to himself what slowly but surely would be his daily rosary: "Let it be what has to be." The agonizing sensation of being in a crossway, in a road with no return, was weighing on him. He either had to kill his godfather or they would kill him; "that simple," had been the words of the Boss. He was facing a serious dilemma.

Slowly, he walked along the streets of the neighborhood uphill; the one of death; the one of the dreams and nightmares; seeking any motive to forget that sorrow that tormented him. It was the first time that he felt his spirit decline before the perspective of an assassination. For Mauro, to kill was business, something with not too many preambles or absurd protocols. It was an act of marketing, where someone paid for a service and he took care of the rest; simple, clean and quick. But with the order received, he had found himself for the first time with something that although he had heard mentioned in the past, never interfered with his professionalism and cold blood: moral. 'Moral' until that moment, had been a strange word but now was drilling his soul. It was the first time that he felt in his interior the need to liberate himself from a battle, in

# PILGRIMS OF DEATH

which he, at the same time, was the spectator and the protagonist. He couldn't comprehend why the balance between good and bad had become part of his priorities.

In the midst of a sunset that showered the buildings of brick and challenging graffiti, he went up to Diana's house; to make things worse, Diana was not there so he didn't know how to release the weight of his oppressed soul. Diana, his forever ex, not even in those melancholic moments was there to soothe that sour flavor or to listen to his sorrows. He felt a slight heat in his cheeks upon thinking that perhaps his mulata of fantasy hips could have been wallowing in bed with someone, and that thought got him more disturbed, since he knew he did not have the right to spy on her after so many years and so many bodies she had enjoyed in his absence.

Sometimes, that city of nightmares, with no respect to their personal beliefs, ages or gender, wrapped up the dreams of its inhabitants and would knead them in a merciless manner, until they became mincemeat; what was peculiar was that the individuals always would recreate their ideals, not minding that a gruesome joke of destiny would give end to their wishes.

# ✠ Pilgrims of Death

It was a constant routine, and in the middle of it was Mauro, always far away from his love, but never far enough as to not to think of a future with her.

He felt a strong impulse to talk to El cacique and he headed towards the butcher shop of his friend and forever protector. As he was going in, he saw his friend closing the shop; he felt he looked older – he seemed to be carrying a heavy load. His walk was slow, when he came forward to say hello to Mauro.

"What a pleasure to see you, man, you had abandoned me. "

"The business, old Cacique, business, but you are nailed in my soul."

"And you are in mine, Mauro. Come in let's have a drink."

Mauro helped close the gray gate of the butcher shop and accompanied him through a small and narrow door which led to the main living room, where they sat comfortably in front of a painting of a great lake and Mauro courteously refused the drink that El Cacique's hand was offering him.

"Well, for what I can see, the matter you're bringing with you is bigger than I thought; "I wonder how things are in hell that it is rejecting souls," he added jokingly.

Mauro got up from his chair and without saying a word, began to do a quick inventory of the simple living room, which had only a pair of chairs, a table, some boxes piled up in a corner, an altar with several images poorly illuminated by a wax candle, a pair of ferns hanging from the ceiling and a light allowing the painting from the lake to be seen in a permanent state of movement.

It was that simple living room the occasion of transcendental reunions and important decisions. There, a while back, peace or war was decided among gangs, sicarios were recruited or weapons and drugs were sold. El Cacique had been the mentor of hundreds of young men who wanted to get out of poverty, putting their lives in the hands of the mafia as long as they could flee from the hole they were living in.

Mauro was sweating rapidly despite the fact that the temperature was pleasant due to a wide open door that lead to the patio filled with plants. The young man closed the only two entrances that the living room had and stood in front of his old tutor, with his eyes distant and red.

# ⁂ Pilgrims of Death

El Cacique observed him with curiosity and thought he was under the influence of some drug.

"I have to kill someone," Mauro said finally.

"And, why so much mystery! Be thankful you have a job; things are difficult lately and to have a commission like that is not a thing to waste."

"That's true, but I don't dare to send to the neighborhood of the dead the one entrusted to me. And if I don't do it, they will kill me," said Mauro with a growing anxiety.

"You're going to have to explain that to me slowly," replied the old man. "When did you lose your balls to take care of a 'simple job'"?

"But you don't understand me; you don't know who we are talking about."

"Although I have a face of a wizard, I am not a magician, and, unless they have paid you to kill me, I don't understand what your complication is," said the man.

"They ordered me to kill Oscar," said Mauro finally.

"And who the hell is Oscar? Do you know how many guys have that name in this city?"

"Oscar, Don Oscar… My godfather," answered

# Pilgrims of Death

Mauro, with an evident tremor in his voice.

The old butcher looked at him with astonishment, and without saying a word, got up from his chair, walked up to the altar and took a bottle of rum from behind the image of an angel with no hands, he extended a glass to Mauro and made a toast in silence.
The air was getting heavier in the living room and one could only hear the agitated breathing of the two men and the crazy dance of the candles, illuminating its owner's illusions. Even the lake in the painting on the wall seemed to have been in the most absolute stillness.
    "That really is a problem, boy," said El Cacique.
Mauro hurried the drink and asked for another which he swallowed with the same haste, for every answer.

That afternoon, Mauro did not leave his friend's home; they drank until dawn and discussed possible ways of action to come out clean from that mess. The hours went by one after another and the spirits of the two friends were appeased but they felt they were going around a circle since they could not find the way to escape. A drink followed another and soon they were listening to music to dissipate the sorrows and deceive the worries.

# Pilgrims of Death

"Look for him Mauro and talk to him. If the Boss already gave you an order, at least show him that you are obeying him and warn Oscar to fix the problem with his brother, don't you think?"

"And if my godfather doesn't want to talk to him? The one that is going to look bad is me," replied Mauro.

"The most important thing is that you respect your word but also your feelings. Look for the answer within you, let your heart be the one to make the decision," the old man concluded.

Daybreak brought with it an incredible hangover but threw over Mauro a light of hope. For the first time, he felt that the most important thing was to be loyal to a friendship, before an order, and with this thought, he got out of the butcher shop staggering not without first giving a strong breaking bones hug to his friend.
He went up to his apartment, slept a couple of hours, and recovered. After a restless sleep, he came out armed with a nine-millimeter pistol, ready to find his godfather.

# PILGRIMS OF DEATH

## THIRTEEN

Jose never knew what took his life; he opened and closed his eyes tenderly as someone who is very sleepy after a long day of playing and study. It was six o'clock in the morning of that Friday when a burning sensation in his neck woke him up; then, everything was silence and peace. The mafia group from the north of the country was more astute than what Oscar had anticipated and when they realized that they had killed the oldest son of their worst enemy, they decided to cease all hostilities and the weave of blood that was vertiginously tarnishing the country so that they could believe that things were already calmed, but while the apparent calm was reigning – making Oscar's nerves and attention relaxed – the capos of the north mafia were moving heaven and earth to find the young man's whereabouts.

They took several days to find a gap in the well established security pyramid of the rival organization, and this was how they found Don Anselmo's ex wife, at last butler of Las Lomas, who was having a dubious affair with a lieutenant of the north mafia, and they did not take long to pressure her to deceive the old man to snatch from him all the information possible.

# Pilgrims of Death

Don Anselmo was a mature and good nature man who had always been in love with his wife, until she had decided to leave his side for a younger man, destroying with her actions ten years of marriage. It only took a week for the woman to get to the top of Anselmo's passions. A promise of eternal love and a couple of million bucks in her bank account were enough to sell her soul to the devil.

Oscar had just left for his weekend get-away, when the organization from the north found out of the loosening and the possible ways of access to the house. On Thursday night, Don Anselmo poured a couple of drinks to the new escorts.
 "Drink these rums, because this is a tradition that the Boss and Don Oscar have to welcome the new body of troops in this house," the old man told them offering each one of them a glass of liquor.

By three o'clock in the morning there was not a single man standing; the sedatives supplied in the rum by the old man had the effect wanted, and in a couple of hours six armored-plated trucks arrived to the place,

## Pilgrims of Death

and no alarm or dog interrupted the reigning tranquility.

One by one the doped bodyguards were riddled, and that's how they got to Jose's bedroom. El *Tuerto*, the boss of that incursion of the north mafia, came to the bedroom, followed by several of his men, all properly hooded with black cowls and armed to their teeth.

One of them had with him a video camera and recorded what later would be left behind as a present for the Boss. El Tuerto, slowly and almost with reverence, approached the boy's bed as he slept placidly on one side; the man looked at the camera, and to make sure he wouldn't be recognized, he posed a tender and overacted kiss, in a giant magnum of German fabrication, while on the other hand he held a picture. Then, he brought the gun closer to the boy's neck and shot, without the minimum tremble in his pulse.

Jose hardly sighed and moved as if a fly had bitten his neck. Following act, the sicario discharged the content

# Pilgrims of Death

of his weapon on the boy's face. The video camera was covered with blood and the men left the place in the same clandestine manner they had arrived.

It had been a perfect plan, where no resistance opposed the avenging force of those assassins. They arrived in the most complete silence, and the same way they left the place, leaving behind the air extenuated with gunpowder mixed with blood.

That same Friday, Oscar was feeling relaxed, after a night of sex and drugs with his girlfriend, and at around ten o'clock in the morning they went out together for breakfast at the swimming pool of the hotel. The resplendent sun of the seashore cleared his senses and he felt like a gallant while he walked around the hotel with his marvelous blonde.

When the phone rang announcing the death of his nephew, he closed his eyes and cried of ire and impotence. His lover asked him what was happening, and he contemplated her silently. Afterwards, he sent her back in the first flight to the city.

He couldn't feel less than depressed and defeated. The difference lied in the fact that now he did not have the moral strength to lead any retaliation because two hours after the fatal news his cell rang again.

"You are no longer my brother, and you should have fallen dead like the bodyguards at the ranch. I'm going to find you and the blood of my son will wash away with yours," was all the Boss said, before hanging the phone leaving Oscar sweating cold in those high seashore temperatures.

He knew he deserved it, but he could not allow his own brother to execute him without giving him time to defend himself. It was his fault; nevertheless, he couldn't surrender without a fight. Several times he tried in vain to contact him; his brother could not refuse to talk to him and search with him for an exit in that labyrinth in which he found himself falling. But this is exactly what the Boss did and never answered his calls.

He decided then, to sneak out of the hotel in the most absolute silence and travel to another city, where he could hide from his brother's wrath. Something inside of him

# Pilgrims of Death

told him over and over again that he was behaving like an ostrich, hiding his head; he was so vulnerable that at every step he felt the whip of his brother's rage over his back.

Money was not the issue, but he was lacking the most minimum to breathe. He was not at peace; he could not trust anyone and he didn't dare to call even his friends or acquaintances; this was how he began a long pilgrimage along the cities in the center of the country. Sometimes he would arrive to an isolated hotel, he would enquire for a room, and if he felt that someone was looking at him in a strange way or would ask him a suspicious question he would go somewhere else, with the same speed in which he had arrived.

These were days of absolute loneliness and skepticism and he mistrusted everything and everyone. In a few days he had become a compulsive paranoid man. When buying the newspapers or upon seeing the news on TV, it did not mesmerize him in the slightest way that his brother had managed to keep in secret the massacre of Las Lomas and the death of his son; but the sea of blood that was showering the country, the bombs and assassinations were up to date. No official authority dared to pronounce judgment over the weave of deaths that devastated the cities. At a great distance one could notice that the powerful mafia groups were avenging themselves, but nobody really knew the reason. The power possessed by the Boss to camouflage the truth was such, and it was precisely that power that made him tremble before the possibility of being found, since he knew that he wouldn't have a trial, or the opportunity to give an explanation or to apologize.

In every city in which he wandered, he would get a new disguise, and would never pay with a credit card or would register under his real name. He avoided the big hotels, and he preferred the distant motels, or low rating lodging houses with an odor of sweat and someone else's sex. He went on a pilgrimage for several weeks, tasting the flavor of defeat, solitude and abandonment. There were many occasions when he attempted to take his own life, but at the last minute he lacked courage to pull the trigger.
Finally, tired of hiding in cities that did not belong to him he decided to hide in his own little terrain; the one who received anyone with open arms and legs … his city, city of no one and everyone. After all, what did he have to

## ⛧ Pilgrims of Death

lose? He decided to take refuge where very few would have looked for him; in the city uphill, that city of those from down the hill because with its characteristics everyone believed that he was in the metropolitan city from downhill, that of the people from uphill. Nobody would dare to think that the Boss's great lieutenant would seek refuge in the miseries of the neighborhood uphill, and this is precisely where he went.

He had a lot of people to go to, among them Mauro, but he knew that his friend owed discipline to his brother, and concluded that the best thing to do was to take refuge in the house of Diana the Diva, ex-girlfriend of his friend and perpetual lover of the organization's lieutenants.

## FOURTEEN

The only thing that relieved Mauro was that he had not been given a deadline to execute his godfather's pending death sentence.

He wandered for several days on his bike, asking the whereabouts of his friend. He looked for him in the city casinos and hotels. He asked the snitchers he knew in other capitals and the answer was always the same negative one with taste of defeat. Nobody knew Oscar's whereabouts; it seemed as if the earth had swallowed him.

There was no corner in the city of opulence in which he did not look for his godfather. He knew him very well and knew what places he used to hang around; this is why he never imagined that it would be so complex to look for a man like him. That city was closing its doors and saw him as a strange and undesirable insect. Now that he walked along the luxurious hotel corridors, without his godfather's company, was when he understood the apathy declared openly to him. Before, people used to bow to almost touching the floor with their foreheads but not because it was Mauro, but because he was in Oscar's company and in that city of

## Pilgrims of Death

brass, it did not matter who you were, only how much you were willing to pay. He traveled to the nearby towns, asking here and there, but he always got the same response... silence, a silence that dashed a sensation of emptiness and discouragement in his heart.

He was able to find out the name of the young blonde who traveled with his godfather to the coastline, and when he learned her address he even went to an upscale residence complex to talk to her. He found himself with the news that she had been found tied up in the trunk of a car, on the way to the airport, with her body riddled with bullets a couple of weeks before. Mauro started to get impatient because he knew that the Boss was waiting for results and although he had been kind to him, he was not a man that you could deceive easily nor solicit to put off 'a job.'

There was not a clue he had not checked, or a hotel in which he had not followed his godfather's trail. He called several of the women whom his godfather used to speak with, and of the few he managed to find (the others did not want to talk to him), he was not able to get anything concise. The indelible stigma of the curse to be wanted by the most powerful man in the country was spreading on the streets like a bad omen.

A clear and starry night, Mauro parked his bike in front of the usual discotheque, and on his way in, *el Cojo* approached him, a likable old man that was famous for selling anything from an electric iron to a gold chain to a grenade. It was said that he was able to sell his soul to the devil, and he, amused, would answer that he was sorry not to believe in that man because happily he would have made a good deal. Mauro greeted him and said he did not want to buy anything.

"Come on, Mauro, buy me that pistol veneered in gold, it belonged to an Arabian chief," said el Cojo.

"A pistol veneered in gold! Where the heck do you get those strange things?"

"Damn Mauro, in this neighborhood of ours one can find anything. In the mud of our streets you can find a rocket-launcher or have a glass of rum with the great Bruce Lee. If John Lennon is alive, he's probably walking through this neighborhood forgotten by the hand of God," concluded the salesman.

# Pilgrims of Death

Mauro did not buy the pistol, but appreciated the conversation; el Cojo went somewhere else looking for another client, and Mauro went in to the discotheque, with his head transformed in a pressure cooker.

Mauro thought that it wouldn't be so absurd, that no one would think that someone important would hide in that low life, dangerous and rugged neighborhood. And what if his godfather Oscar would think the same? Since he started his search, it had never occurred to him to look for him there; the bad reputation and easy bullets sector was not a place of Oscar's caliber. The great bosses of his organization used to go up there sporadically to recruit sicarios or to create panic among the deserters or snitchers, but this was probably why this was the perfect place to hide and to be unnoticed since nobody would've thought of looking for him in that place.

While he rushed a beer and rejected an invitation to dance, he began to make a list of the people that knew Oscar and of those that his godfather would trust. After his fourth beer, the circle was narrowing down to two people whom his godfather would blindly trust in case

# Pilgrims of Death

he needed help; Diana and himself.

But if after so many days following the death of his Boss's son, his godfather hadn't looked for him, the chances were he wasn't going to do it now. And as far as Diana was concerned, she was a good candidate to earn Oscar's trust, since they had known each other for many years and she had an overwhelming list of contacts in the underworld, leaving aside the love affairs of his ex with the lieutenants of his godfather's organizations.

He had been looking for her for many days to talk, but she did not show any signs of wanting to talk to him. Mauro became impatient, and rushed his fifth beer. Then he left the place with the intention of finding out if his guesses were only echoes in his head or realities in front of his nose.
If for an instant, he had imagined that his ideas would take him to the doors of a reality showered in blood, perhaps he would have preferred to leave that city forever.

# Pilgrims of Death

### FIFTEEN

The morning that Oscar knocked on the door of Diana's house, he did it dressed as a beggar and Diana's first answer was to send him to hell for having woken her up. What a nerve and petulant way of begging at seven o'clock in the morning! The young lady was furious when she noticed that the beggar didn't change to her impudent remarks and was offering her a nice smile that did not match his ragged resemblance.

The young woman approached the window one more time and observed him closely. Oscar winked his eye and pointed to the entrance in the most complete silence. Diana ran toward the door, and scared and complacent opened it. It had been weeks since she was not visited by Oscar, and that was a very lucrative pleasure for her.

Diana jumped onto his neck; Oscar kissed her rapidly and tenderly. He asked that they go to her room; she though his behavior was very strange since at times way back when, when he would solicit her *services*, he would order someone to bring her to one of his apartments but he had never asked her to receive him in her bedroom.

# PILGRIMS OF DEATH

"I'm messed up. I'm in the middle of one of the biggest problems you can imagine, and it occurred to me to only ask you for help," said Oscar with a couple of tears on his face.

One could notice the tiredness of long nights of insomnia and over his body the eternal hours of suffering were taking its toll.

In very brief words, Oscar told her everything that had happened on those days, and Diana became astounded with the news that his back had become a point of reference to play target shooting. Diana gave him a glass of orange juice and caressed his hair tenderly. Due to Oscar's indifference, she understood that he was there for something totally different than sex, so she decided to move quickly.

"My cousin Olga is on a trip and I have the keys to her apartment. It is not a big deal and it's located few blocks from here; if you'd like, we can go there right now."

"Perfect! It's fine with me, and I think it would be a good idea not to stay in your home," replied Oscar.

In less than half-hour they sneaked out clandestinely toward the place proposed by Diana. They walked to

# ✠ Pilgrims of Death

the place and got in without problems.

The apartment had two floors, was being repaired, disorganized and poor; but it camouflaged perfectly with the neighboring buildings and for such, it wasn't noticed.
Oscar looked through the first floor window to make sure that no one had followed them or that any indiscreet look would threaten his plan of being unnoticed. The peace on the street brought him a little tranquility.
The main living room didn't have a lot of commodities; four chairs and a wicker table, a big crucifix and a radio. Down the hall, one could see a little kitchen. On the second floor, there was only an ample bed and a couple of guitars on the floor. It looked more like a second-class motel than a family home, but compared to what this man had suffered in the last couple of days, this was a paradise.

Oscar could not resist but to watch the provocative curves of the young woman as she pulled down the curtains from the second floor.

"Are you still Mauro's girlfriend?"
"No, but we see each other frequently and we

seem like a couple although we're not; it so happens that between Mauro and I exist something stronger than a magnet… I think that if destiny exists we're going to grow old together. Why is that important?" asked the young woman.

"Under other circumstances… none, but with everything that's happened to me, and keeping in mind how much Mauro loves you, the best thing is for us to behave like friends, don't you think?

"It's ok with me," answered Diana, in the midst of disillusionment and agreement.

"Don't feel bad, Diana, you've always been one of my favorites, the fact is that I have let down many people and wouldn't want to let both of you down," said Oscar. Diana did not quite understand the man's behavior but she thought it to be very gentleman-like that he did not look for her to simply have a romantic session home delivery.

"So, now what?"

"To wait, just to wait," said Oscar.

"Have you spoken to Mauro? Maybe he can help you."

"I haven't talked to him for more than a month, and I'm afraid that I can't look for him because it is possible that my brother has hired him, knowing that he knows me well," he said with a tiring tone.

"Mauro could never fail you."

"Mauro is one of the best, he is a professional, and until I find out that he has not been hired to act as my brother's vengeance's arm, I can't trust him," Oscar sentenced, with a cloud of worries in his eyes.

They talked for a long time, in which Diana swore to keep quiet the secret of his whereabouts and not to reveal to anyone what was happening within the criminal organization. She returned to her home and in less than one hour she was back providing Oscar with a small arsenal, which contained a couple of fragment grenades, a machine gun and a revolver.

"I don't know how to pay you for this favor Diana."

"Keeping yourself alive and trusting me; that is how you can pay me," replied the young woman.

## SIXTEEN

About one month before, when Oscar was wallowing in bed with his girlfriend and his sicarios were being decimated without resistance, Don Anselmo thought he would soon be able to re-establish his home and flee the country with a juicy amount of money in his pocket. He never kept in mind that the mafia does not pay with conventional clauses of businesses.

Anselmo gave the signal to the men who were waiting few kilometers near the farm, and as soon as he saw the escorts that guarded the house fall down under the effects of the sedatives, he felt proud that everything would work out according to the way it was presented to him.

Once the vans with the sicarios arrived, the massacre began. Anselmo directed the man with a red bandana in his left arm, exactly as it had been ordered to him the day they agreed on the plan; that was the only way to distinguish the head of that operation with the rest, because all of them had their faces covered. He took him through the stairs that led to the second floor, followed by a handful of men.

At the front door of Jose's bedroom the commander ordered quietly to two of the sicarios to remain in the corridor guarding Anselmo, which seemed exaggerated

# Pilgrims of Death

to him, but after all, he did not want to see what was about to happen inside.

Seconds later, Anselmo could not feel less than a contortion in his stomach, upon hearing the first shot coming from the young boy's bedroom followed by many more. Then, a crushing silence impregnated the walls and his heart.

All had ended and now he could leave that place to meet with his woman, to forgive his faults and to wash them off with liquor, with the best rum available in the market, because that was the reason why, as of that night, he had become a millionaire.

The bodies of the bodyguards were still warm, when a body of troops of the Boss arrived. More than two hours had gone by and no one had reported by radio. They were supposed to communicate every hour as it was ordered, and due to the silence the Boss sent a backup group which only found the blood and silence.

The men cadavers were everywhere, close to them there were empty glasses; every skull showed a bullet impact; a precise and only shot, which made the deaths appear as an execution, not as a shooting. The men's weapons had not even been pulled out and none had been fired that night. All the dogs were dead; they had a viscous drooling in their mouths.

*El Mono,* commander of that rescue incursion, began to sweat cold, in front of what seemed by all evidence, the kidnapping of Jose. But his spirit went down even further, when he found the body of the young boy riddled with bullets on his bed; he could bet that it was him, although the shots impacted on his face had left a distorted mass and it was difficult to see the former beauty of the boy.

El Mono ran to the monitor room, camouflaged in the miniscule bedroom next to the living room on the first floor, to find out why none of the alarms had been activated. The room had been carefully manipulated and put out of order, by someone who definitely knew the house security systems because all the cables were disconnected or cut, leaving the infrared systems and video cameras inactive.

The cadaver of a man was found leaning on the control table; it was the only body that had been shot on the back. Upon getting closer they could see that it was Anselmo, the butler. Besides the shots on his back, his jaw was out

# Pilgrims of Death

of place and one could see in it a plastic bag that contained a videotape. It was protected carefully by an impermeable material, and the traitor's teeth were clutching to the tape like a dog on his bone.

Hours later, the Boss would be watching with his eyes coming out of their sockets, the only thirty five seconds of recording found in the video, where the pupils of a man seen through a black hood, who then kissed the pistol that blinded his son's life forever and that irrevocably sentenced his brother, since the killer that executed Jose, held in one of his hand the photo of two women; they were the aunt and sister of the second north mafia capo, whose deaths opened a caudal of blood and the end of the cold war between the groups.

## SEVENTEEN

Finally, Diana showed interest to speak to Mauro and asked him to meet her at *Doña Susa's* Cafeteria.
Mauro's persistence had been such, that the young woman felt strange by the coincidence to say the least, because she herself was looking for him.

Mauro placed a tender and brief kiss on Diana's lips – it had always been that way –their hands sweated upon shaking and their eyes danced in front of each other's figure. It seemed as if they'd never had separated.

Mauro invited her for an afternoon snack and ordered some biscuits. He took Diana's hair in his fingers, but did not dare to say a word. When he had the sodas in front of him, he offered one to Diana; she looked at him tenderly and murmured:
"Like old times."
"Yeah... and for old times' sake" said Mauro, at the same time that they toasted.

They looked like a pair of adolescents in a romantic rendezvous. There were no remains from the bully and the woman with doubtful reputation. They transformed themselves upon being in front of each other. They remained like this for several minutes, in mystic

# Pilgrims of Death

contemplation, without rushing, without being ashamed, without cover ups and with lust. They drank their soda without hesitation and talked about the latest gossip in the neighborhood; the deaths in the city were endless and she asked if they were keeping him busy with *jobs*.

Mauro cleared his throat, and for the first time in the whole conversation he could not resist the intense blackness of her stare.

"Did you hear about the bomb at the school?" Asked Mauro, trying to evade the issue outlined by Diana.
"Yes, something very big must've happened in order for them to be breaking their souls and be destroying the city. But I asked you if they had given you a contract to participate in this *party*."

Mauro looked at her with affection and kissed the palm of her hand. A weave of her perfume penetrated his senses, and made him evoke so many nights of passion with that woman who taught him the path of love and hate.

# PILGRIMS OF DEATH

He needed to find a way out of that evasive game to approach the subject which had pushed him to look for her.

"Have you found out anything about my godfather?"

"About Oscar?, Why? What's going on..."? replied Diana.

"No, it's nothing, what's happening is that for several days I haven't heard from him, and since this is becoming very dangerous, I was asking myself what's going on with him; that's all."

"Mauro, you cannot lie to me. I know you as well as I know myself. What is really happening to you? Why the urge to talk to me and what's the reason for not answering what I asked you regarding whether they hired you to be part of these killings?"

Mauro swallowed saliva; the precision in which Diana talked left him astonished. He only dared to look at her, and he melted in front of her presence.

Diana took his hand and scrutinized him with her gaze, then, she put her hand through the disorganized hair of the young man and sat up over the table to give him a kiss.

"Mauro, in this neighborhood one can no longer live, and we're too old to play mouse and cat. Whatever truth we're hiding from each other would only bring more blood. You are the best, the one that everyone fears, but I know that the one with the most fear is you. Let's talk openly to each other and let's see what can be done, don't you think? "

An unwanted sigh came out of Mauro and he had to make a big effort to not begin to cry in front of her. She had touched a very deep fiber of his intimacy and she was right. He submerged in those night–color eyes, and taking a deep breath, he said:

"The Boss ordered me to kill my godfather."

Diana looked at him in silence and perceived the terrible internal struggle that the young man was freeing himself of at that moment. She took a peaceful attitude, although she knew the big problem she was into because upon collaborating with Oscar, she was challenging his brother.

# Pilgrims of Death

"That's awful. But both of them are *blood!* What do you plan to do?"

"I don't have the slightest idea. For now, try to look for him and talk to him," replied Mauro.

"Are you looking for him to talk or to do your *job?* The nights of insomnia and the moral problems that had been outlined all those days of search, appeared reflected on his face for a second; the dilemma about the friendship, the loyalty and the duty seemed to have found a firm port in front of the eyes of that woman with cinnamon skin.

"No, my love, how can you think that? I love my godfather very much and I need to talk to him. I have never complained about the jobs from the Boss; it is the same to me to send to the cemetery an old lady or a doctor. I only have to be told whom to 'knock down' and it's done; I am not one to ask questions... But in this case, they moved the ground under me and I am petrified because if I don't kill my godfather, they will kill me," said Mauro, with a desperate tone, caressing with force the hands of the young woman.

# ⚔ Pilgrims of Death

"And do you know why the Boss wants him killed?"

"It seems that it has to do with the death of Jose... but I don't know anything else."

Diana remained for a long time assessing the conversation and comparing the facts that had been given to her by Mauro and Oscar days before. She came to the conclusion that both of them needed to have a dialogue and tell each other their side of the story, and then the rest would come.

"What do you think?" asked Mauro, with growing nervousness.

"And if I tell you that I know where your godfather is, what would happen?" inquired Diana.

"I had already thought about it; something told me that he might have asked you for help... What would happen? Then, I would appreciate it if you'd put us in contact or you can tell him to call me; I need to talk to him."

"Mauro, after all we've been through, you and I have always loved each other, right?"

"Yeah, but do you think that this is a good moment for declarations of love, my darling?" gladly answered

## Pilgrims of Death

Mauro.

"I only want you to promise me that if I find the way to get you together, you're not going to do anything to him; you're only going to talk, right?"

"My love, you know that I wouldn't break a promise to you; I could be a bad guy, but I would never do anything bad to him. I am a man of my word, and I give you mine. Before I do anything, I will talk to my godfather."

"What do you mean 'before you do anything? Does that mean that when you see him, you'll greet him very nicely and then you'll blow his head off?"

"Diana, my love, I don't have any intention to mess up with the few principles I have left. My godfather is like the father I never had. I need to talk to him to try to resolve things, but after that, God will decide."

"Ok. Let him be the one to decide."

"So, are you going to tell him to call me or are you going to tell me where he is?"

To answer him, Diana took him by the hand and invited

## Pilgrims of Death

him to leave. They paid the bill, and hugged each other before crossing the street. Mauro was very restless with Diana's mystery, but upon feeling the waist of the young woman near his side, he began to relax.

They greeted el Cojo, who was on the other side of the street, near the neighborhood's pawnshop. The old man had become a type of good luck charm for the neighborhood. The old man gave him a signal with his thumb up in the air and invited Mauro to embrace Diana; his scarce dentures, dismantled by the years, shone, just before disappearing in a cloud of smoke.

When the explosion of the bomb was heard, Mauro, with his feline reflexes, threw Diana to the floor and covered her body with his. It took only a fraction of seconds, and the pawnshop along with el Cojo disappeared forever from the neighborhood.
That's what the city had become: a time bomb. The hour, the place or the fallen ones didn't matter. Little by little the neighborhood, the city and the country were becoming a gigantic agonizing animal that was losing blood every second.

# PILGRIMS OF DEATH

And the indifference was so amazing that people were no longer shocked to see human remains flying until landing on roofs or on trees; life had to go on, and that seemed to be the way assumed by the actors of that tragedy.

The car parked in front of the business, that had lodged the explosive freight was disseminated all over the block. A piece of metal had fallen near Mauro's body. They got up cautiously, and upon making sure that they were ok, Diana thanked her gentleman with a kiss, while they got away from the place with the memory of el Cojo making signals of victory before his death.

Diana trembled; although she lived in that jungle of cement and lead, she had not been able to get used to all of that. She knew well that the city had already reached a vegetative state, where indifference was the shield, but she still kept sensitivity before those acts.

A thousand thoughts went through Mauro's head, but the one he could not dispose was the feeling of pity for his neighborhood in pieces, bleeding excessively by diabolic and merciless machinery.

# Pilgrims of Death

Those impressions never went through his mind; he only worried about coming out of it unharmed, everything else was not important; at that moment while he ran with his mulatta by his side, he thought of how sad it was to see the face of death, and to continue to be dauntless as if his capacity of astonishment had been extinguished as the vapor of a dream.

## EIGHTEEN

Mauro was astonished by Diana's audacity to hide his godfather in the neighborhood, in the heart of poverty and violence. He walked to her cousin's house and Diana explained the details of Oscar's arrival soliciting her help, days before. Upon arriving to the house, the young woman reminded him again of his commitment to talk to him and not commit any crazy act. They went in the house promptly and they closed the door behind them. Mauro was impatient; he was sweating not being able to hide his nervousness when Oscar came downstairs from the second floor, and remained in the corridor observing them.

The three of them remained still looking at each other for seconds that seemed like an eternity. The sun filtered through the only window of the room and reflected over the furniture of the place, the silhouettes of the individuals present worn by work. The reigning silence was broken every second by external noises although Mauro believed that his heartbeat was the loudest of all. Mauro examined his godfather with a quick look, and he found him thinner, with black eyes and a tiresome appearance.

# Pilgrims of Death

He looked unarmed and did not show a warlike expression. Once again, he felt two forces pushing inside of him: The one indicating that he should shoot on the spot, and the other one that struggled to take afloat the sensitive and dignified man he had inside.

"Well, now that we're together, would you like a beer?" exclaimed Diana breaking the silence.

The men did not answer. Mauro walked to where Oscar was and immediately Diana nervously cleared her throat. The young man did not pay attention to that. The young woman thought she was not seeing well, when she observed that Mauro, the tough guy, the neighborhood thug, the seven lives, jumped over Oscar's shoulders, in a strong embrace covered with tears. Precisely with this embrace, the gentlemanly behavior, the honesty and loyalty triumphed. In that greeting, the seed of hope was planted. Not everything was lost in that jungle of cement. Those warrior hearts were laying the foundation of a tomorrow without violence, without deaths, where hatred would only be a memory, a bad memory.

# Pilgrims of Death

Oscar received the hug with pleasure, and he could not withhold some tears that revealed the state of commotion in which he was in. Diana looked at them astounded; it was like seeing two rough wrestlers, mellowed by a rose and a poem.

"Ok guys, don't cry anymore that you're going to ruin my make up" said Diana satisfied and hugging at the same time the two men.
"Godfather, it's so good to see you."
"You mean "it's so good to see me alive,"" joked Oscar.
"Yes, it's true; the way things are I was imagining the worse."
"Things couldn't be worse, right Mauro?"
"Yes, godfather, they are worse than you can imagine. Your brother ordered me to kill you."
Oscar looked at him with admiration, and immediately hugged him again with a paternal expression. Mauro asked Diana for coffee instead of a beer and the two men sat down.

# Pilgrims of Death

"I had imagined it; my brother knows that you are indeed the best, and it pleases me that he hired you, otherwise, I would have felt offended."

"But the fact is that I cannot kill you, godfather, and I don't know how to get off my back that responsibility. You know the Boss and he already sentenced me; besides, I don't know why he wants to blame you for Jose's death."

"I'm guilty of having been careless with him and I made enormous strategy mistakes in order to please my weaknesses. Now I cannot do anything because I can't even talk with my brother."

"But why does he say that you are guilty of your nephew's death when I am a witness of the fact that you adored Jose?" asked Mauro restlessly.

A pause was made when Diana came back, and the three of them drank coffee; between sips, Oscar told Mauro the whole truth of his trip to the seashore, and his direct responsibility for that act that brought death to his nephew and several of his men.

Although Oscar was not aware of the details of what happened or of the existence of the video with the death

## Pilgrims of Death

of his nephew, he assumed that something much more powerful exalted his brother's state of mind as to only want to see him dead.

Mauro listened attentively to the story of what happened about the days of escape and loneliness that his godfather had undergone, until Diana interrupted the story.

"I understand that your brother loved his son very much, but it's odd that he doesn't at least want to talk to you. You are the same blood, and it can't be that for only one mistake, the Boss would dirty his hands with his own family, without giving you the opportunity to defend yourself."

"My brother is a very powerful man, his children are his most precious treasure and for them he is willing to do anything; for him family is the most important thing as is the organization. Before this fatal mistake, I was the one that put in jeopardy his whole institution and the stability of the entire city," said Oscar sadly.

"Come on godfather, you know the job; you couldn't have put in danger the peace of the country and of the organization."

"Maybe it's necessary that I tell you from the beginning."

# Pilgrims of Death

It was like this how Oscar related what happened months before, in the attempt on the building where it was presumed that the collection of sport cars of the boss of the north mafia cartel.
Oscar, as his brother's lieutenant general, had as mission to make presence of the power of his organization all over the country. Hours before the explosion, one of the bodyguards informed his doubts to Oscar about the location of the building, making it clear that the place where the cars were was somewhere else. Everything was already perfectly coordinated by Oscar and the car bombs that would detonate were in place, besides, he had a trip to Aruba in a matter of hours with a couple of astonishing brunettes, so he didn't have time to correct any mistakes and he ordered to continue ahead with the plan.
The last information was correct, and in the building in question there was no car collection and it wasn't empty; on the contrary, families and friend of the bosses of the north lived there. This caused the war to begin and the tacit agreement of the cold war was forgotten. Mauro and Diana looked at each other and did not find a way to continue the dialogue; it was Oscar who broke the sticky silence.

"As you can see, it was my mistake that awoke

the cholera of our enemies. My brother had been forceful in maintaining an agreement of no aggression and no intromission in the business between the two organizations, and although we've always considered them as enemies, he came up with a strategy so that each group could take care of their business without interfering with each other, until I *screwed up,* and they took it against our people. And to make things worse, I screwed up again when I should've protected my nephew, and therefore, don't be surprised that he, even being my brother, has ordered my execution."

"I am very sorry about what I'm about to say, but that womanizer habit of yours does not have God's forgiveness," exclaimed Diana.

A doubt floated in Mauro's head. Now that he knew what had really taken place, and his godfather had somehow confessed his responsibility of the events, should he pull the trigger?

Oscar seemed to guess the thoughts of the young man because he decisively looked at him and said:

"Don't worry Mauro, it is not your fault that you've been ordered to kill me."

# Pilgrims of Death

### NINETEEN

They spent that night talking, and neither of the three slept. Frequently, they looked out the window, but the neighborhood was very calmed and it seemed to be reposing with tranquility.

At dawn, the decided to change houses and Mauro proposed that they go to an empty apartment that belonged to his friend el Cacique.

"He's trustworthy," he said.

The hours went by and the memories began to flourish in their minds; very soon they were talking with fluency and almost with impudence of the thousands of misdeeds they had lived together.

The sunrise was waking up the roosters of the neighborhood, and the first lights began to clear, inundating the streets of hope. Mauro asked his godfather not to go out; that he would take care of organizing everything and that within few hours he would return.

"Be very careful," asked Oscar.

"Let be whatever has to be, godfather" replied the young man.

Then, he gave Diana a sounding kiss and he disappeared in the labyrinth of the streets of the sector. Mauro felt confident, but strangely, not for the fact of being armed; he felt his soul lighter. He was in a good mood, he had passed a very tough test by facing and confronting his godfather; the rest would come alone. Besides, he didn't believe that the Boss would follow through with his word of killing him, since he had waited a long time and he had not attempted until now. through with his word of killing him, since he had waited a long time and he had not attempted until now.

His thoughts had him abstracted from reality, and he was not appreciating his neighborhood's sunrise, its colorful inhabitants, and neither the animals announcing the new day.

Upon turning around the corner where the butcher shop was located, just imagining, he began to savor the delicious coffee that his friend would prepare for him.

He arrived at the entrance of the house and he pronounced the name of his friend. A hoarse silence answered back. He called again, and when he did not get an answer, he pulled out his weapon and entered the hallway secretly.

The brightness of a light illuminated half way the darkness and Mauro understood that it was from the

# Pilgrims of Death

candles that daily illuminated his friend's altar. He didn't have to call the butcher again because he found him sitting in the chair where days before he was lecturing Mauro.
A waive of ire ascended up to the young man's cheeks, making him breathe in with pain. The man he was looking for was immersed in a river of blood; his chest had repeated perforations and his crystallized gaze showered the place. He had a piece of sky blue cloth tied around his neck. He approached the body and he closed his eyes.
"See you later old man, let there be what has to be," said Mauro as a way of farewell.
He turned off the candles and got out of the place running. In his desperate escape, he did not take any precaution, and it did not occur to him that the Boss' men would have the guts to attack him; "not for now," he thought.
He ran as if possessed, and a couple of blocks further he realized he still had his weapon in his hand. He put it away and tried to calm down but he was only interested in talking to his godfather and making sure that all was in order with them.

# Pilgrims of Death

Before knocking at the door, Diana who was already looking through the window had opened it.
"Now we really have to go any place," said Mauro out of breath.
He explained what had happened, and nervousness took over them. A couple of minutes went by before anyone could react and it was Oscar who spoke.
"Let's wait until the end of dawn and we'll look for another hiding place, but the most important thing is to call my brother, I'll try to make him respond; I've got nothing to lose by trying.

" At around eight o'clock in the morning, they decided to go down to the discotheque to see what kind of mood was there. Their intuition told them that they should go separate ways and on foot; after all, it was only a couple of blocks away. Diana would go in front of Oscar to show him the way. They took with them few of their belongings and they loaded their weapons.
Diana looked through the window and said that there was no one suspicious. Mauro opened the door, and in fact confirmed that there was not even a soul on the street, which seemed very strange to him because at

that time many children used to go by, coming down from the hills to the school or workers to their jobs, but on the street there was not even a dog or a fly breaking the peace.

In an instant, the deafening noise of a couple of motorcycles crossed the air, and Mauro did not have a chance to finish the sentence:

"To the ground!," when they were already receiving a shower of machine guns, that shattered over the house without compassion.
Each motorcycle had two passengers and each one worked his weapons mercilessly. Through the half-open door Mauro was able to shoot, and one of the killers felt like a bag on the sidewalk from across the street. Another biker, upon seeing his partner fall, and that the targets were responding to the fire, lined up his motorcycle down the street, and the second motorcycle followed him immediately.

Mauro got up from the floor, and after confirming that his godfather was okay, he ran to where Diana was lying. He called her and since he did not hear her answer, he turned her over, and saw her smiling. A thin thread of blood bathed her forehead.

"Give me a kiss, Mauro, and behave yourself", Diana whispered. Mauro hugged her with strength, and Diana's body, his mulatta, the woman of his dreams, his passionate Goddess, diluted in his arms with a sigh. The images of his life and passion went before the eyes of the young man, who was not able to believe that his only love expired in front of him, without being capable of doing anything to remedy it.

Oscar remained standing, astonished, without daring to pronounce a word.  He shook with anger, withimpotence, and placed a hand over Mauro's shoulder. The latter cried over the lifeless face of the only woman he had loved; a caudal from his eyes bathed the coldness that began to reign in that beautiful body.
The light filtered through the orifices that had ploughed the bullets in their dance of death, and outside one could not hear anything, not even a curious person, or a police . . . nothing.  It seemed that the neighborhood confabulated against them, giving its back to his sons.

# Pilgrims of Death

The two men looked at each other and understood that they could not waste any time, because if the Boss had decided to take matters in his own hands, there was very little they could do to avoid more bloodshed. They had to leave this place as soon as possible.

And it was this way how with deep sorrow, he abandoned the house, leaving behind Diana's body.
"It's my fault," said Oscar.
"Maybe is everyone's fault, for having gotten into this life of hatred and blood," replied Mauro, dedicating his last look to Diana.
They came out of the house and confirmed that the killer that was dead on the sidewalk belonged to theBoss's gang which did not surprised them in the minimum. Mauro was tempted to empty the remaining of the bullets in his pistol on that disarmed body, but he thought that this wouldn't please Diana.

They ran several streets up to where they saw a vehicle parked and nobody near. Mauro opened it with the experience only gotten by street smarts and they left without definite course.

## Pilgrims of Death

Since they did not have a place to go, any place was a good one but they decided not to get more people involved and they went to a second class hotel in the outskirts of the city. They requested a room with a view of the street but decided to stay for a moment in the main lobby. Mauro looked at his godfather, encouraging him to do what he needed to do. Oscar agreed and walked towards a public phone.

# Pilgrims of Death

### TWENTY

At the other end of the phone line and of the city, the voice of the escort and Boss's secretary told Oscar to wait. Despite the place being cool and ventilated, Oscar sweated profusely.
A couple of endless minutes went by, before he could hear the hoarse voice of his brother.
"What do you want?"
"Hi, I only wanted to ask you to listen to me and to put an end to these killings," Oscar dared to say.
"You are in no position to ask for anything. You already lost the opportunity to be heard."
"How is Viviana?" Upon hearing the name of his daughter, he couldn't avoid but to suffer a light shiver; he was a witness of the tremendous affection that Oscar professed over Vivy.
"Fine, but you don't care about that anymore. What did you call for?"
"If what you want is my life, I'll give it to you myself but let's not make our own people kill each other," Oscar begged.
"And do you think that I'm going to listen to a Don Juan, a *playboy*, who was the reason why my son was assassinated? Look Oscar, if it wasn't for those

sick desires of yours to mess around with any woman, maybe you had committed less mistakes and Jose would be at my side at this moment."

"I recognize my mistake and ask your forgiveness..."

"May God forgive you because I lost my patience to support your faults," replied the Boss with a tone of contained ire upon hanging up the phone.
Mauro, who had listened to the conversation from Oscar's side, only had to make a small effort to imagine the other side of the conversation, since he only had to see his godfather's facial depressive expression.
Through the open door of the hotel, a soft breeze was coming in and inundated the room where the two men were looking at each other with sadness; they felt defeated and trapped.

"Why don't you do what you were ordered to do, and we finish once and for all with all of this?" asked Oscar.
Mauro looked at him as if it were the first time; in front of him, there was a gigantic fern that seemed to be dancing over his wide back. He tried to respond, but the noise of a car, instinctively made him look toward the door; it was only a vehicle that was passing by the place

# Pilgrims of Death

at a great speed, and the two men could not avoid their laughter due to the nervous wreck they had become. Mauro got a knot in his throat upon remembering the day that Diana introduced them, and he had to make a big effort in order to hold his tears at that instant. He evoked pleasant moments he had experienced thanks to his godfather's favors: money, women, drugs, games, trips; all seemed so remote, that the young killer could only breathe, when he began to talk to Oscar.

"Finish once and for all with what, godfather, your life? I could've shot you right in the head when Diana took me to the place you were hiding in. I just needed a couple of seconds to send you to the world of the dead and maybe she wouldn't be dead. But who assures me that once I had killed you they wouldn't have come to finish me?"

"Well, you're right. You know that my brother likes the jobs well done and you took a long time to obey him," said Oscar.

A fat woman, with a tobacco smell, approached them and offered them coffee. They received it and didn't talk until she had gotten completely away leaving a trace of stale smoke on the air.

# Pilgrims of Death

"Godfather, it was very hard for me to listen to what the Boss had to say, but understand that one cannot disprove him. I thought it was something for the spare of the moment, and that his anger toward you would go away. I don't have brothers but I imagine that blood carries weight, don't you think?"

"Yes, but I don't blame my brother; because of my fault he lost his own blood and there's a limit to tolerate the mistakes."

"Don't get sad godfather, we cannot afford to distract ourselves now," Mauro comforted him.

The hours slowly went by and the two men talked more relaxed, observing the nature that filled the hotel surroundings.

The light was starting to fall over the hills and the darkness began to reign around the place giving lead way to a spectacular concert of crickets and cicadas. From the hill where the hotel was located one could appreciate the city in all of her splendor. The door and all the windows showed the lights of the metropolis that witness with hope the birth of the infants and observed death with despair. How many conflicts,

# ✠ Pilgrims of Death

hunger, victims, dreams, tears and smiles sheltered that city that was ready to go to sleep? Nobody knew, not even those two men that were watching the sunset with ecstasy. They had undergone such tough moments; they knew death so closely, that they felt strange to be feeling sensitive as they contemplated that sea of concrete expanding under their feet. They felt nostalgia for having been participants of so many massacres; they had forgotten to love that city that saw them grow up for so many years, that now they debated unusual thoughts, which brought them to believe that the time to pay for their faults was near. Mauro noticed that for a long while they had not seen the woman with the tobacco smell and no one from the hotel. In addition to this, no vehicle had broken the silence on the street. He told his godfather and immediately they became alert; they made an inventory of their weapons which were not many, since they hadn't had time to go to Mauro's house for more. Therefore, they only depended on Mauro's pistol and on the ones that Diana had given back to Oscar. An accomplice stare made them feel like *kamikaze;* they laughed upon feeling the same as crazy suicidal, trying to stop with so few weapons the Boss's fury.

"What is the expression that you normally say, Mauro?"

"Let it be whatever is meant to be."

"Ok." And he repeated the sentence at the same time that he loaded his machine gun.

"It's okay, godfather, but I have done so much harm to so many people that I don't believe he will have mercy on me."

"Don't talk nonsense, Mauro that God always is with you, no matter how bad you've been."

"Well then, like my aunt used to say: "May God protect us", because this is going to be rough."

"Amen, Mauro, and thanks for having such a big heart."

"Don't make me be sentimental, that my eyes will get watery again, and we need all the aim of the world at this moment," said Mauro with a humorous tone.

"Aim. . ? My god, boy, against my brother we don't need aim; what we need is a miracle.

# ⚜ Pilgrims of Death

## TWENTY-ONE

Mauro wasn't wrong. So much tranquility was only the prelude of a storm. The street in front of the hotel began to fill up with blinded vehicles with polarized glass; it seemed like a funeral parade.
There were no motorcycles rubbing their tires or vehicles going one hundred miles per hour. No, all of them came as if they were parking for a funeral, without rush, without any commotion.
Oscar looked behind the hotel, and was able to see through a window that it was full of armed men who, in a relaxing mode waited in position covering all exits of the building. They seemed to understand the enormous disadvantage that the people from the hotel had and the orders had been very precise: "No one shoots until I order it." The Boss himself had taken charge of the operation and everyone waited on his decision.

"Ok godfather, the time has come to wait for a miracle because from this one we won't escape."
Both embraced each other quickly, signaling a farewell and they placed themselves in front of the hotel windows. They knew that they were vulnerable there, but at least they could give it a good fight before falling because they did not intend to surrender to be executed

# PILGRIMS OF DEATH

without compassion. At least, they wanted to give themselves the pleasure of dying under their own law, which made them famous in the gangs of the underworld.

No one got off from the blinded cars and no one seemed to be anxious to begin the shooting. Silence could be touched with the hands and everyone was asking themselves how long would the torture last. Suddenly, the sound of a helicopter was heard landing slowly on the parking lot of the hotel, and all eyes were on it. That was why Oscar and Mauro were some of the best assassins remembered by the city because their cold blood did not move them to even open fire at the slightest movement.

From several blinded cars, four men descended with machine guns and approached the chopper. All of them had a blue ribbon on their left arm. The doors of the chopper were opened and two escorts descended. Seconds later, the Boss himself came down, and behind him his secretary.

Even the crickets seemed to understand the seriousness of the situation because they ceased their singing and one could only hear accelerated heartbeats. The Boss in person was there. He was wearing a neat black suit

# ⁊ Pilgrims of Death

and a red tie; and around his left arm he wore the same distinctive as his bullies. He did not have his dark glasses with him, which usually accompanied him and his resemblance was stern. Mauro did not give any credit to his eyes; this was not normal behavior and he did not know how far he would go with his presence there.

The group of men surrounded their boss, and walked a couple of yards, until they were far away from the vessel. The Boss's face was rigid, sad; he projected the sensation that he was attending his own funeral. He walked slowly, floating on the pavement, approaching his destiny with no rush.

The bodyguard that played the role of secretary had a deep scar on his left cheek and on his right hand a black briefcase. Upon a signal, the man came close and opened softly. The Boss pulled out from it an extraordinary nine-millimeter silver pistol and with no expression on his face, he loaded it.

The Boss looked toward the entrance of the hotel, and settled his eyes on the windows. There he noticed Mauro's head, and observed it without suspicion, taking his time to breathe and think.

Mauro returned the look as if apologizing, but he

# PILGRIMS OF DEATH

couldn't avoid allowing flashes of cholera and his inflammable wishes to revenge the death of Diana and his friend el Cacique to be unnoticed.

Several feet away from there, his brother got a knot in his throat and a thread of sweat blurred Mauro's vision.

The Boss searched at the other window, and discovered Oscar's eyes scrutinizing him without blinking. For a couple of seconds, each brother's stare weighed up the other. It was never known what went through the minds of the two men, but everyone present was lit up by the eternal stare between them.
Nobody knew for sure what the Boss' plans were but it was clear that the ceremony of the silver pistol and his mere presence in the place had all the characteristics of an execution tailored to his style.

With a decisive but slow pace, the Boss walked to the hotel entrance, while the pistol shone in his hand; then, whatever seemed impossible occurred.

# ᛋ Pilgrims of Death

## TWENTY-TWO

When his secretary handed his cell to him, the Boss gave him a withering look; the man apologized, but insisted that he needed to respond. He himself had given orders to have calls from his daughter directed to him at whatever time day or night. He had a single phone line just to assist her because due to the critical situation in the city he was afraid that something could happen to her.

When the phone rang, everyone present jumped remaining alert, but no one moved from their places. The secretary answered the call and immediately handed the device to the Boss.

The men that walked next to him stopped walking while the latter listened to Vivy's voice.
The image froze completely, all the men were ready for any order given and one could only hear a slight whisper from the man, while he answered the call.

The Boss – the toughest and the most powerful man in the country – was settled in the middle of the parking lot, in the midst of his hatred for his brother and his daughter's voice.

# Pilgrims of Death

He didn't dare to hang up or to continue his Calvary to the hotel. He was there, immerse between two currents that pulled him with impetus.

The man hung up the phone, returned it to his secretary and everyone waited for the order to restart the march. He, always so placid and methodical, remained silent while a drop of sweat faded near his tie.

He didn't say anything; he didn't pronounce a syllable. He remained for a long time looking at his brother's pupils, and without a grimace he threw his silver pistol toward the door of the hotel that upon falling produced a deep and swift sound that diluted in the eardrums of those present; following this, he turned around and got on the helicopter, while he gave a couple of instructions.

When the pistol provoked that sound on the ground, a wave of faults to expiate woke up in Oscar's soul. The echo of the falling pistol resounded in the most intimate of his soul's sorrows, and he felt guilty again for being irresponsible and a womanizer.

# Pilgrims of Death

In less than a minute, all the men and the vehicles disappeared from the place, leaving behind them a cloud of dust and emptiness. Nobody spoke; no vengeance was uttered; no shot was fired; all was left in silence, such a sticky silence that obstructed breathing.

On the entrance's asphalt, the silver weapon shone; it was the only proof of the presence of the assassins in that place.

Mauro could not believe his eyes; he was watching Oscar who was trying to find an answer to what happened but this one shrugged his shoulders as perplexed as him. When they assured themselves that it had nothing to do with a trap and that they were alone, they breathed with a sense of relief.

"What happened?"

"I'm not sure, maybe the miracle we were waiting for," Oscar replied.

Mauro cautiously came near the hotel entrance, and picked up the pistol that was shining in the darkness. The two men contemplated it admiring its beauty. Oscar claimed it extending his hand, and Mauro gave it to him.

## Pilgrims of Death

"This was… is to purge my mistakes," Oscar sentenced. Mauro did not add anything but did not like the lugubrious tone that his godfather had used.

# ⳨ Pilgrims of Death

## TWENTY-THREE

Several months had gone by since the night at that hotel, and Mauro could not free himself from the sensation that a much too powerful force had intervened at that time.

He lamented and suffered a lot due to the loss of his Mulatta; it had been devastating to his heart to have seen his Diana disappear, but he could not revive her now, and by a very strange reason, he also did not feel any desire to revenge her death.

Hours later, that night in the hotel, after the unexplainable departure of the Boss, Mauro and Oscar said farewell to each other and took two different paths. Upon embracing, Oscar said with a serious tone of voice:

"Take care of yourself, Mauro, and forgive me for what happened to Diana and for everything. Absolve me because I can't do it myself."

"Godfather, don't talk nonsense, that what happened was meant to be; take care of yourself and please call me."

# PILGRIMS OF DEATH

If Mauro would have known that that was the last time he was going to see Oscar, prehaps he would not have permitted the separation.

Oscar put the silver pistol inside his shirt and gave Mauro the other weapons. They looked at each other again, and Oscar added:
      "There's no doubt you are a character, thank you!"

Mauro did not say anything; he remained in the middle of the parking lot wrapped in a cloud of darkness and anxiety. He waited for the taxi that he had called and left that place forever; the next day he also left the city. It hurt him to leave behind his neighborhood of sorrows, loves and joys, but he felt he needed to hide away for sometime. He was very wrong in this because contrary to all things expected, there were no retaliations from the Boss; he was never wanted again nor did he feel followed. He was not able to understand his attitude, but he had the premonition that something too powerful had occurred with that phone call that spared his life.

# ⚰ Pilgrims of Death

After a while, he returned to his city with the intention of speaking with his godfather, and the outcome hurt him, but this was the last thing he did there before leaving for good to try his luck in another country.

Oscar, two weeks after the incident at the hotel, was able to talk to his niece Viviana, and understood what happened after she made a call to her dad, when, by an act of coincidence o providence, she could not contain the impulse to phone her dad to ask him about his uncle Oscar. The night before, Vivy had had a nightmare where she saw her father throwing her Uncle Oscar through a precipice subjugated and tied to snakes and to a gigantic sword that brandished the emptiness leaving her incapable of doing anything to stop the fall of her favorite uncle. In the dream, the girl cried and screamed inconsolably while no one could hear her. She spent the whole day agitated and nervous, so she decided to call her father to tell him the strange nightmare and begged him to always protect Oscar... Her cries were heard in the phone line, right at the moment when a miracle was needed.

# Pilgrims of Death

Oscar understood the importance of that message, thanked and said good bye to his niece… forever.

He divided all his properties, the ones that were *clean* in the eyes of the law, between Mauro and Viviana. Of course, Mauro did not receive a penny from that inheritance, since there were mechanisms and laws more efficient to divert confiscated moneys than to catch criminals.

He went to the Lomas, which was uninhabited since the massacre that ended Jose's life, and he shot himself in the head with the silver pistol.

Mauro: a lucky charm, a relic, clownish or womanizer; a murderer or altar boy, disappeared in a strange country, changed his name, and life style. He became a walking memory, a perpetual sorrow in the post evocation of his city, its sorrows and joys. He changed his life but in his soul permanently fixed he carried the sorrow of what life had taught him there far away in the neighborhood up on the hill that after all, was the neighborhood of the people down the hill.

# ACKNOWLEDGMENTS

In order to make a reality this edition of Pilgrims of Death, the energy and talent of people whom, more than being resources I consider friends, came together. It is thanks to them that these ideas crafted on paper are able to enter your soul today and acquire life of their own.

A well deserved and especial acknowledgment to Fernando Martinez, my friend and advisor.

To the Creative Talents of Arturo Velasquez & Gloria Porras, I owe the graphic design and photos of the cover.

To my two musketeers Mone and Nando, who have always trusted my writings

To the talent of bilingual poet Maria Flórez at the time of translating this novel, and to Edward Ortiz for his straight forward comments at the time of reviewing all texts.

And to my longing city of Medellin; manipulated, blemished, but always haughty and manorial; which knew how to teach me the hardness of death and th tenderness of forgiveness with the same amount of patience and tenacity.